AN EXPLORATION OF ALICE WALKER'S MASTERPIECE
THE COLOR PURPLE

DR. SHAHIN FATMA & DR. FOUZIA USMANI

VOICES IN VIOLET

BLUEROSE PUBLISHERS
U.K.

Copyright © Dr. Shahin Fatma & Dr. Fouzia Usmani 2025

For permissions requests or inquiries regarding this publication, please contact:

BLUEROSE PUBLISHERS
www.BlueRoseONE.com
info@bluerosepublishers.com
+4407342408967

ISBN: 978-1-0369-0655-9

Cover design: Daksh
Typesetting: Tanya Raj Upadhyay

For permissions requests or inquiries regarding this publication, please contact:

BLUEROSE PUBLISHERS
www.BlueRoseONE.com
info@bluerosepublishers.com
+4407342408967

ISBN: 978-1-0369-0655-9

Cover design: Daksh
Typesetting: Tanya Raj Upadhyay

First Edition: January 2025

Table of Contents

Chapter-1 Reclaiming Voice: The Color Purple as a Cornerstone of African American Literature 1

Chapter – 2 Intersectionality of Race, Gender, and Class: A Womanist Reading of The Color Purple 18

Chapter- 3 Understanding Race, Ethnicity, and Family Life 27

Chapter – 4 Violence of Language 54

Chapter – 5 Eco-Womanism in Alice Walker's Works: Intersections of Gender, Race, and Ecology. 83

Chapter- 6 The Dawn of Independence 98

Bibliography 139

Chapter-1
Reclaiming Voice: The Color Purple as a Cornerstone of African American Literature

African American literature is a genre of literature that deals exclusively with African Americans. This literature originated in the United States and was spread throughout the world by writers who were mostly of African descent. The genre goes back to the eighteenth and nineteenth centuries, with writers such as Phillis Wheatley, Frederick Douglass, and Olaudah Equiano, who wrote about their experiences as slaves. During the 20th century, writers such as W.E.B. DuBois and Richard Wright explored themes such as cultural isolation and Black Nationalism during the American Civil Rights Movement.

African American literature holds a significant place in world literature today, highlighting the experiences of people of African ancestry in the United States. The genre explores themes of justice, liberty, custom, slavery, and experience, and often includes folklore, oral poetry, music, rap, and blues. The genre has been subject to debate, with some academics including non-black characters, leading to a paradoxical situation. Prominent writers in the genre include Toni Morrison, Zora Neale Hurston, Maya Angelou, and Paule Marshal. Early African American literature was written during the periods of slavery, and writers such as Phillis Wheatley, Frederick Douglass, and Olaudah Equiano highlighted the atrocities of slavery. During the 20th century, writers like Toni Morrison, Zora Neale Hurston, Alice Walker, and Richard Wright wrote on themes of racial discrimination, African society, and Black Nationalism. The literature of African Americans exists due to the differences in their history and experiences compared to the rest of American culture. Slave narratives, religious redemption tales, and tales relating to abolition and progress are some of the essential components of African American literature. Commenting on African American women writers, Mary Helen Washington writes, "I realize that black women writers are an important and comforting presence in my life. Only they know my story *(Introduction. –A Women Half in Shadow*, p-13). Prominent writers of African American literature include William Brown, Jupiter Hammon, Victor Sejour, and Gustavus Vassa. African Americans had a significant impact on American literature, and their literature has become known worldwide. It has contributed to the understanding and appreciation of African American history, culture, and social issues while serving as a tool for promoting diversity and inclusion in society. African American literature has also inspired movements for social justice and civil rights and has encouraged the emergence of new voices and perspectives in literature. Today, African American writers continue to produce works that address diverse themes such as identity, gender, sexuality, class, race, and intersectionality. Their literature offers a unique lens through which we view and understand the experiences of African Americans and the complexities of American society as a whole.

The most important movement of this era the Harlem Renaissance marked a pivotal moment in African American literature. This movement saw black authors and artists exploring racial identity and pride in their works. One of the era's most celebrated writers was Langston Hughes, who wrote about the black experience in a way that was accessible to all. Hughes's poetry, which contained everyday language and was often set to music, became a key component of the Harlem Renaissance. Other notable writers of the era include Alice Walker, who wrote about the unique experiences of black women, and Richard Wright, who explored themes of social injustice and inequality. In recent years, African American literature has continued to evolve and adapt. African American writers such as Ta-Nehisi Coates and Jesmyn Ward have won acclaim for their works, which explore contemporary issues such as police brutality and the aftermath of their retaliation. These writers continue to push the boundaries of African American literature, engaging with new themes and experimenting with new forms of storytelling. African American literature is a rich and diverse genre that has evolved to reflect the changing experiences of black people in America. From the earliest works of Phillis Wheatley and Fredrick Douglass to the contemporary writings of Ta-Nehisi Coates and Jesmyn Ward, African American literature has provided a platform for black voices to be heard and for their stories to be shared with the world. Despite the many challenges they have faced, African American writers have continued to inspire and empower others, using their words to create a better, more inclusive world. Their works serve as a testament to the resilience and creativity of the African American community, and their contributions have enriched not only American culture but also the literary canon of the world. As we continue to grapple with issues of race and inequality, African American literature remains a vital tool for understanding the

From slave narratives to contemporary bestsellers, African American literature has always been a powerful medium for expressing the struggles and triumphs of black life in America. Many great writers have emerged from this tradition, including Langston Hughes, Zora Neale Hurston, Richard Wright, James Baldwin, Toni Morrison, and Maya Angelou. Their works speak to the experiences of black Americans, from the horrors of slavery and segregation to the ongoing fight for civil rights and equality. They offer insights into the unique challenges faced by the black community, and provide a means of understanding the importance of cultural identity and heritage. Despite the different forms of slavery practised Toni Morrison strongly opposed chattel slavery prevalent in society. According to Keith& Cartledge of all the forms of slavery, chattel slavery was "The most extreme form of un-freedom form in antiquity in which the slave was conceptualized as a commodity, akin to livestock, and was owned by a master who had full capacity to alienate his human property, by sale, gift, bequest, or other means" (*The Cambridge World History of Slavery; The Ancient Mediterranean World. Vol. I, p- 112*).

African American literature is also a tool for breaking down barriers and promoting understanding between different communities. It invites readers to explore the complexities of black life and culture and to grapple with the history and legacy of racism in America. According to Stuart Englishmen, "Blackness suggested connections with the Devil. Africans were regarded as heathens, which made them seem barbaric to many Western Europeans" (Kopytoff& Miers 2, p- 83). However, in the contemporary world, as we face ongoing challenges around issues of race and inequality, the importance of African American literature only grows. By telling the stories of the black experience, these writers continue to inspire and empower generations of readers and promote greater understanding and empathy among all people. Moreover, African American literature reminds us of the beauty and resilience of black culture and the many contributions that black Americans have made to our society. It helps to lift diverse voices and to challenge stereotypes and misconceptions. According to Potter Abbott, "Narrative is the representation of events, consisting of stories and narrative discourse. A story is an event or sequence of events (the action) and narrative discourse is those events as represented"(*The Cambridge Introduction to Narrative. Cambridge*, p-16).

In the 1960s, race, rather than gender, was the major cause of subjugation for blacks. In the words of Heuman and Trevor, "The black woman was deprived of a strong black man on whom she could rely for protection" (*The Routledge History of Slavery, p- 212*). The society lacked political presence, coupled with the despotism of alternative voices, which led to the rise of Black Feminist Literature. The white liberal feminist movement lacked the audacity to highlight the issues confronting black writers. Human rights activist Malcolm X, in his autobiographical book *The Autobiography of Malcolm X* (1965) described his deteriorating family condition. The tradition of incorporating autobiographical writing into African American literature had its beginning with the publication of spiritual autobiographies during the mid-18th century. As said by Clair Janet, "White, as well as black spiritual autobiographies, commonly contrast some form of physical captivity with spiritual freedom" (The Courageous Undertow of Zora Neale Hurston's *Seraph on the Suwanee, Modern Language, p*-13). Following the preliminary political unveiling by the previous writers as Jupiter Hammon and Phillis Wheatley, the chief fictional appearance adopted by the Negro was the slave narrative. The most eminent writer of the age was Gustavus Vassa, an African of Nigerian origin. These measures served as a means of accomplishing the propagation of their narratives in the United States. The free Africans of the North, along with the escaped slaves of the South, made a strong impact and aggravated the conscience of the nation.

Slave Narratives as a Subgenre of African American Literature emerged in the middle of the 19th century. According to Kopytoff &Miers, during the period of the Atlantic slave trade, around "10 million Africans crossed the Atlantic during the period of the slave trade" (*Slavery in Africa: Historical and Anthropological Perspectives, p-32)*. The debate over slavery revealed the many facets of slavery. The menaces of slavery were explicitly depicted in books, and one such example was *Uncle Tom's Cabin* (1852), which proclaimed its abolition. However, the Whites named it "Anti-Tom Literature." The pro-slavery was explained by writers such as William Gilmore. The perils of this curse had cast black wings on society, prompting the slaves to write their own stories. These slave narrative fictions served as the backbone of African American literature. Approximately six thousand slaves from various parts of Africa, especially the Caribbean islands and North America, wrote chronicles of their miseries and pain as slaves. These pieces were later published as pamphlets and separate books. The narratives of the slaves are broadly divided into three different forms. The first category includes tales relating to religious redemption, tales relating to the abolition of slavery, and tales relating to progress. These tales personify conventional features that aim to stimulate the audience violently by quoting their life as examples. This writing by African Americans was considered the most valuable contribution of the age.

Constant endeavor demanding the eradication of slavery eventually led to its eradication. However, this made little difference to the plight of African Americans. The African American authors continued writing about the miserable condition of this section, portraying their grievances even though slavery and the American Civil War had finally come to an end. According to Paul Lovejoy, "Slavery is a form of exploitation that is common in most societies and most historical periods" (Burnard &Heuman 06). Another prominent writer was W.E.B. Dubois. He is widely known for founding the NAACP, an association for the advancement of colored people. His book, *The Souls of the Black Folk,* is a collection of essays on race born out of Dubois's own experience. His writing exemplifies the position of African Americans in American society. He attempted to call on all African Americans to unite together and raise their voices against their prevailing situation. Contrary to his ideas, Booker T. Washington (1856-1915) espoused a more demanding project for his people toward ending racial discrimination. According to him, blacks must learn to promote themselves and place themselves on a pedestal similar to whites. Being an educator, Washington led the foundation of Tuskegee Institute, a college for blacks in Alabama. Some of his remarkably renowned narratives were *Up from Slavery* (in 1901), *Tuskegee and its People* (in 1905), and *My Larger Education* (in 1911). Marcus Garvey, a journalist, writer, and campaigner for Black Nationalism led the campaign "Back to Africa Movement". The main goal of this campaign was to persuade people of African descent to return to their ancestral homeland.

Despite these challenges, African American writers have made invaluable contributions to literature, using their unique perspectives and experiences to offer powerful insights into the human condition. They have challenged established norms and ideologies and helped to expand our collective understanding of what it means to be human. As readers, it is our responsibility to actively seek out and promote the work of African American writers, to provide them with the platforms and support they need to succeed, and to challenge the systemic barriers that have prevented their voices from being heard. Ultimately, recognizing, supporting, and amplifying the voices of African American writers is essential if we are to build a truly inclusive, diverse, and equitable society. Their work has the power to challenge our assumptions, broaden our perspectives, and inspire us to create a more just and compassionate world. The Harlem Renaissance was a movement that transformed the African American community by uplifting artists, writers, and musicians. Harlem, New York City, became the black capital of America during this period, with writers, painters, sculptors, and playwrights presenting their innate talents with much passion. The movement had an enduring effect on the vibrant black urban culture, empowering the American Civil Rights movement and profoundly impacting black writers of the 1940s, 1950s, and 1960s. Despite the tremendous achievement and advancement, the movement failed due to the lack of financial support received by the artists.

The Black Ghetto was yet another attraction for the diverse collection of white celebrities. By identifying equally with the Negros, the revolutionaries defied their own culture and background. Some were too affluent to work yet were unable to add any benefit to society due to a lack of education. The majority of these professional outcasts were Negros who had become estranged from their families and homelands while attending college. Their immense suppression and turmoil anxiously waited for a chance to vent out their embedded emotions of resentment and anger. Their white masters helped them by providing them with a subsidy until they mastered the skill. However, the experience of these encampment followers was never written. However, these small ventures contributed significantly to the rise of the New Negro Literary Renaissance. The pioneers of the Civil Rights Movement also produced books and essays that emphasized human rights. The latter phase of the Second World War saw active African American writers turning their ability to activities relating to hostilities in the war. A new generation of African American writers surfaced after the death of Richard Wright, with writers like Frank London Brown, William Melvin Kelly, and Paul Marshal challenging the previous interpretation of African American life. Famous writers during this period include James Baldwin, Richard Wright, Ralph Ellison, Zora Neale Hurston, Alice Walker, and Toni Morrison. African American poets have also attracted audiences from around the world through their writing, with Rita Dove winning the Pulitzer Prize and serving as the country's Poet Laureate from 1993 to 1995. Playwrights August Wilson and Ntozake Shige were also notable for their plays, with both winning Pulitzer Prizes for their work.

The literature on African Americans is used both within and outside of America. African American literature is considered by critics to be a component of the Balkanization of American literature. The artistic patterns of African American culture, jazz, and hip-hop gained immense popularity, attracting crowds and stimulating American culture. While the movement failed in terms of being financially sustained, its impact on African American culture, society, and literature continues to be felt and celebrated today. In addition to writers, musicians and artists also played a pivotal role in the Harlem Renaissance. Jazz music, in particular, became a defining element of African American culture during this time. Musicians such as Duke Ellington, Louis Armstrong, and Bessie Smith gained widespread acclaim and helped to break down racial barriers through their performances. Visual artists also had a major impact on the movement, with painters like Aaron Douglas and Jacob Lawrence capturing the spirit of the Harlem Renaissance through their vibrant and expressive works. Sculptors such as Augusta Savage and Richmond Barthé also gained recognition for their contributions to the movement. Today, the legacy of the Harlem Renaissance can still be seen in modern African American literature, art, and music. The movement catalyzed change in American society, paving the way for future generations of black artists to express themselves and assert their cultural identity. While it may have failed in some respects, the Harlem Renaissance remains an important milestone in the history of African American culture and a testament to the power of artistic expression. The 1960s and 1970s were a crucial time for African American identity. The division of the unified community marked the beginning of various small communities. The rise of Black Feminist Literature was a result of the lack of political representation in the mainstream feminist movement and the subjugation faced by black women.

Alice Walker was a literary giant of the African American community who celebrated black folk culture and black life. Her works are a true reflection of African American culture and folklore, which provided a glimpse into the lives of the black community. The most diverse aspect of African American literature is depicted in its fiction, and Alice Walker stands out in the era due to her immense contribution. Her works were able to conceptualize the multifaceted aspects of life prevalent in the Afro-American setting, which was unique at that time. The extensive literature written about Walker's life and works has helped in understanding African American literature better, providing a new direction and dimension to the subject. Her contribution to African American literature cannot be overemphasized. Her works portray a realistic and honest picture of black people and their lives, which was not previously explored. Walker paved a path for other female African American writers to express themselves and their experiences. Her works are not just literature but a true reflection of African American culture and folklore, which provided a glimpse into the lives of the black community.

Alice Walker is a celebrated African American author, poet, and activist, best known for her groundbreaking novel The Color Purple. Born in 1944 in Eatonton, Georgia, Walker's writing is deeply influenced by her experiences growing up in the segregated South. As a vocal advocate for civil rights, women's rights, and social justice, she uses her work to explore themes of race, gender, and identity. The Color Purple earned her the Pulitzer Prize and the National Book Award, cementing her place as a key figure in American literature. Through her work, Walker has provided a powerful voice for African American women and their struggles for empowerment. The Color Purple is a profound and transformative work in the landscape of African American literature, earning its place as one of the most important novels of the 20th century. Published in 1982, it tells the story of Celie, an African American woman who endures years of abuse and oppression but ultimately rises above her circumstances to find her voice, reclaim her dignity, and experience personal freedom. Set in the early 20th century in the rural South, Walker's novel captures the intersection of race, gender, and class, giving voice to the struggles and triumphs of African American women who had often been marginalized in both literature and society.

The narrative unfolds through a series of letters written by Celie to God and, later, to her sister, Nettie, allowing readers to intimately experience her pain, growth, and resilience. Walker's use of dialect and vivid, sensory language draws readers deeply into the world of her characters, while the themes of sisterhood, spirituality, sexuality, and empowerment resonate universally. One of the key features of The Color Purple is its portrayal of African American women's experiences, showing them not only as victims of societal and familial oppression but also as agents of change, capable of immense strength and transformation. Walker's exploration of the bonds between women—whether through friendship, family, or love—serves as a powerful counterpoint to the patriarchy and racism that define much of Celie's world. Through the relationships Celie builds with figures like Shug Avery and Sofia, the novel reflects the healing power of solidarity and personal growth.

While The Color Purple has been lauded for its bold exploration of sensitive issues, including sexual violence and racial discrimination, it also serves as a testament to the capacity for love and human connection to transcend even the deepest trauma. As such, the novel is not just a critical piece of African American literature but a timeless narrative about the human spirit's resilience and its unyielding desire for freedom, justice, and equality. Through its gripping story and richly developed characters, The Color Purple remains a cornerstone of African American literature, challenging readers to confront both the historical and contemporary struggles of African American women while celebrating their strength, survival, and triumph.

Works Cited

Abbott, Porter H. *The Cambridge Introduction to Narrative. Cambridge* University Press, 2002.

Bradley, Keith, and Paul Cartledge. *The Cambridge World History of Slavery; The Ancient Mediterranean World. Vol. I.* Cambridge University Press, 2011.

Douglass, Frederick. *Narrative of the Life of Frederick Douglass: An American Slave. Anti-Slavery Office, 1845.*

Dubois, W.E.B. *The Souls of the Black Folk. Cosimo Classics, 1903.*

Equiano, Olaudah. *The Interesting Narrative of the Life of Olaudah Equiano or Gustavus Vassa.* Printed for, and sold by the author, 1974.

Haley, Alex and Malcolm X. *The Autobiography of Malcolm X* 1965. Penguin Books, 2001.

Heuman, Gad an,d Trevor Burnard. *The Routledge History of Slavery.* Routledge Press, 2010. *Colonialism/Postcolonialism.*Routledge Press, 2005.

Hughes, Langston. *The Big Sea.* Hill and Wang Press, 1940.

Jones, Sharon L. *Critical Companion to Zora Neale Hurston A Literary Reference to her Life and Work.* Facts on File, 2009.

Re-reading the Harlem Renaissance: Race, Class, and Gender, Greenwood Press, 2002.

Kopytoff, Igor and Suzanne Miers. *Slavery in Africa: Historical and Anthropological Perspectives.* The University of Wisconsin Press, 1975.

Sejour, Victor. *Le Mulatre*. Bissette, 1837.

Walker, Alice. *The Colour Purple.* Harcourt Brace Jovanovich, 1982.

A Cautionary Tale and a Partisan View. Women's Press, 1984.

Washington, Mary Helen. *Introduction.–A Women Half in Shadow.* In I Love Myself When I Am Laughing and Then Again When I Am Looking Mean and Impressive: A Zora Neale Hurston, Reader. Ed. Alice Walker. Feminist Press, 1991.

Wells, Ida B. *Crusade for Justice: The Autobiography of Ida B. Wells.* University of Chicago Press, 1970.

Chapter – 2
Intersectionality of Race, Gender, and Class: A Womanist Reading of The Color Purple

Alice Walker's *The Color Purple* is a landmark in African American literature, engaging with issues of family, identity, race, and gender. To appreciate Walker's contribution, one must examine the historical trajectory of African American literature, which emerged in the 18th century with figures like Lucy Terry Prince and Phillis Wheatley. This tradition, rooted in narratives of slavery and freedom, evolved into powerful articulations of Black life, encompassing themes of resistance, community, and personal dignity. In the 19th century, authors like Harriet Jacobs and Harriet Wilson addressed Black women's struggles, portraying themes of sexual violence and motherhood within slavery. Harriet Jacobs' *Incidents in the Life of a Slave Girl* particularly explores the struggles of enslaved women, addressing themes of sexual harassment, abuse, and the fight to protect their roles as women and mothers (Jacobs 42). These early works paved the way for 20th-century explorations of African American identity, resulting in authors like Alice Walker, who redefined Black women's literary voices through themes of womanhood, race, and survival.

Walker's life experiences shaped her literary vision. Raised in a sharecropping family under Jim Crow oppression, her parents resisted racist expectations, instilling in her a fierce sense of dignity. Her mother's refusal to submit to white supremacy is echoed in Walker's characters, who confront personal and systemic oppression. As Walker recalls, a plantation owner once told her mother that Black people didn't need an education, to which she retorted, "You might have some Black children somewhere, but they don't live in this house" (*The Color Purple* 250). Walker's literature, spanning poetry, novels, and essays, focuses on Black women's endurance in a racist, sexist society. She emphasizes relationships over historical events, portraying women's collective strength and the importance of spiritual and creative resilience. Through *womanism*, Walker highlights Black women's agency and critiques both racial and gender hierarchies.

In *The Color Purple*, Walker dismantles patriarchal structures, portraying female protagonists who journey from fragmentation to empowerment. Celie's initial oppression is evident in her stepfather's warning: "You better not never tell nobody but God. It'd kill your mammy" (*The Color Purple* 1). This silence, enforced through violence, is emblematic of broader societal oppression. Walker critiques male dominance but also portrays male characters capable of transformation, suggesting the possibility of healing fractured relationships. Barbara T. Christian notes, "Walker's women seek connections that transcend blood ties and redefine family as chosen networks of love and support" (Christian 42). Walker's works are grounded in African American oral traditions, spiritual narratives, and a deep reverence for the earth and ancestral heritage. She skillfully weaves personal experiences with broader cultural symbols, reflecting on collective trauma and resilience. The matrifocal focus, evident in *The Color Purple*, underscores the vital role of women in cultural continuity and survival. As Gloria Joseph explains, "Black women often carry the heaviest burdens in family life, suffering in silence to keep the family unit intact" (Joseph 76).

Her critique extends to racial injustice and colonialism, highlighting the global dimensions of Black women's struggles. Nettie's letters from Africa reveal, "Africans are not like us. They think we crazy to try to live like white folks" (*The Color Purple* 163). Cheryl A. Wall states, "Walker expands the discourse of race to include colonial encounters, reminding us that racism is a global system" (Wall 89). Through *The Color Purple*, Walker offers a nuanced portrayal of Black life, capturing its pain, beauty, and hope. She advocates for a feminist vision grounded in community, empowerment, and love, making her work a crucial voice in both African American and feminist literary traditions.

2.1 Family: A Site of Both Oppression and Healing

In *The Color Purple*, Alice Walker presents family as a dual space of oppression and healing for Black women. Celie, the protagonist, experiences intense familial abuse, symbolizing the intersection of gender and racial oppression. From the outset, her stepfather warns her into silence: "You better not never tell nobody but God. It'd kill your mammy" (Walker 1). This brutal line reflects the systemic silencing of Black women within patriarchal family structures. Similarly, Sofia's account of lifelong struggles underscores pervasive gendered violence: "All my life I had to fight. I had to fight my daddy. I had to fight my brothers. I had to fight my cousins and my uncles" (Walker 39).

However, the family also becomes a space of healing and solidarity. Celie's relationship with her sister Nettie offers her emotional sustenance and hope: "Dear God. Dear stars, dear trees, dear sky, dear peoples. Dear Everything. Dear God" (Walker 192). Nettie represents a moral anchor, helping Celie envision a world beyond her abuse. Moreover, the sisterhood among Celie, Shug Avery, and Sofia creates a form of a chosen family. Mary Helen Washington observes that "the bonding of women is not merely an act of resistance but a celebration of their collective power" (Washington 104). Thus, Walker's narrative transforms family from a site of trauma to a space of empowerment and mutual care.

2.2 Racial Discrimination and Its Implications

The Color Purple vividly depicts the pervasiveness of racial discrimination in the lives of Black women. Sofia's violent encounter with white authority reveals how racism shapes their experiences. When Sofia refuses to become the mayor's wife's maid, she is brutally assaulted: "The polices come, start slinging the children off the mayor's wife, bang they heads together" (Walker 85). This moment demonstrates how white supremacy is violently enforced, particularly against defiant Black women. Furthermore, Nettie's letters from Africa expand the discussion of racism to a global context, reflecting colonial exploitation. Nettie writes, "Africans are not like us. They think we crazy to try to live like white folks" (Walker 163), indicating the cultural divides intensified by colonialism. Cheryl A. Wall argues that "Walker expands the discourse of race to include colonial encounters, reminding us that racism is a global system" (Wall 89).

Bell Hooks further contextualizes this in her analysis of Black women's oppression: "The racism Black women experience is often inseparable from gendered subjugation, making their oppression doubly intense" (*Ain't I a Woman* 52). Thus, Walker's work captures the multifaceted nature of racial discrimination and its destructive impact on Black women's lives.

2.3 Intersectionality of Race, Gender, and Class

In *The Color Purple*, Alice Walker explores how race, gender, and class intersect to shape Celie's life, reflecting Kimberlé Crenshaw's theory of intersectionality. Celie embodies multiple marginalized identities, suffering as a poor, Black woman subjected to systemic violence and neglect. She recognizes her social position when she states: "I'm poor, I'm black, I may be ugly and can't cook... But I'm here" (Walker 187). This line encapsulates Celie's awareness of her compounded oppression. Crenshaw argues, "The intersectional experience is greater than the sum of racism and sexism" (Crenshaw 1244), a concept fully realized in Celie's experiences. Her journey to independence reflects resistance to these intersecting forces. By establishing a sewing business, Celie gains economic autonomy: "I got my own house. My own land. My own sewing machine. And I am happy" (Walker 192).

Patricia Hill Collins underscores the significance of economic empowerment: "Economic independence is a key factor in resisting oppression and redefining Black womanhood" (*Black Feminist Thought,* 117). Walker portrays Celie's evolution from a victim of intersectional oppression to a self-reliant individual, demonstrating the power of resilience and agency.

2.4 Womanism: Community and Empowerment

Walker's concept of *womanism* is integral to *The Color Purple*, emphasizing Black women's solidarity and empowerment. Through her relationships with Shug Avery and Sofia, Celie discovers strength and self-worth. Shug advises Celie, "You got to git man off your eyeball, girl. You got to let him know who got the upper hand" (Walker 115), urging her toward independence and empowerment. Walker defines *womanism* as "A woman who loves other women, sexually and/or nonsexually. Appreciates and prefers women's culture, women's emotional flexibility... loves struggle. Loves the Folk. Loves herself. Regardless" (*In Search of Our Mothers' Gardens* xii). This philosophy is reflected in Celie's transformation from a submissive figure to an assertive, independent woman.

Mary Helen Washington notes, "In Walker's vision, the bonding of women is not merely an act of resistance but a celebration of their collective power" (Washington 104). Ultimately, Walker presents womanism as a path to healing and self-discovery, grounded in community and mutual care. Celie's declaration, "I'm here" (Walker 187), becomes an affirmation of life, survival, and empowerment.

Conclusion

The Color Purple is a testament to the resilience and strength of Black women. Walker addresses the critical issues of family violence, racial discrimination, and systemic injustice. Her womanist approach emphasizes the healing power of community and self-love, offering a vision of liberation grounded in shared experiences. As Walker affirms, "One thing I try to have in my life and my fiction is an awareness of and openness to mystery, which to me, is deeper than any politics, race, or geographical location" (*The Color Purple* 10).

Works Cited

Collins, Patricia Hill. *Black Feminist Thought: Knowledge, Consciousness, and the Politics of Empowerment*. Routledge, 2000.

Crenshaw, Kimberlé. "Mapping the Margins: Intersectionality, Identity Politics, and Violence against Women of Color." *Stanford Law Review*, vol. 43, no. 6, 1991, pp. 1241–1299.

Hooks, Bell. *Ain't I a Woman: Black Women and Feminism*. South End Press, 1981.

Walker, Alice. *In Search of Our Mothers' Gardens: Womanist Prose*. Harcourt, 1983.

Walker, Alice. *The Color Purple*. Mariner Books, 2003.

Wall, Cheryl A. *Changing Our Own Words: Essays on Criticism, Theory, and Writing by Black Women*. Rutgers University Press, 1989.

Washington, Mary Helen. "The Darkened Eye Restored: Notes toward a Literary History of Black Women." *Black American Literature Forum*, vol. 16, no. 3, 1982, pp. 98–104.

Chapter- 3
Understanding Race, Ethnicity, and Family Life

> Saturday morning Shug put Nettie letter in my lap. Little fat queen of England stamps on it, plus stamps that got peanuts, coconuts, rubber trees and say Africa. I don't know where England at. Don't know where Africa at either. So I stir don't know where Nettie at. (102)

The quote above highlights how Celie's limited awareness of the broader world emphasizes her role as the novel's primary narrator. Her struggle to understand the contents of the envelope reveals her inclination to view events through a personal lens, focusing on immediate concerns like the whereabouts of her sister Nettie rather than broader political or geographical contexts. This personal perspective underscores the emotional intensity of Walker's narrative of not only sexual oppression, but it also introduces a critical tension between personal and public themes in the novel. Critics have debated how Walker's emphasis on Celie's domestic viewpoint affects the novel's treatment of Race and Class. Lauren Berlant, argues a separation of "aesthetic" and "political" discourses in the novel and concludes that Celie's narrative ultimately emphasizes "individual essence in false opposition to institutional history" (868). Similarly, George Stade critiques the novel's "narcissism" and its "championing of domesticity over the public world of masculine power plays" (266). Conversely, Elliott Butler-Evans appreciates how Celie's letters highlight a "textual strategy by which the larger African-American history, focused on racial conflict and struggle, can be marginalized by its absence from the narration" (166).

In summary, while the novel's intimate portrayal of Celie's life provides powerful insights into sexual oppression, it has also been criticized for potentially limiting its exploration of racial and class issues, leading some to question whether the text's domestic focus diminishes its engagement with the collective struggles of black people. Thus Butler-Evans finds that Celie's "private life preempts the exploration of the public lives of blacks" (166), while Berlant argues that Celie's family-oriented point of view and modes of expression can displace race and class analyses to the point that the "nonbiological abstraction of class relations virtually disappears" (833). And in a strongly worded rejection of the novel as "revolutionary literature," Bell Hooks charges that the focus upon Celie's sexual oppression ultimately de-emphasizes the "collective plight of black people" and "invalidates ... the racial agenda" of the slave narrative tradition that it draws upon ("Writing" 465). In short, to many readers of *The Color Purple*, the text's ability to expose sexual oppression seems to come at the expense of its ability to analyze issues of race and class.

An analysis of race representation in the novel reveals a deeper insight: Walker's expertise with the epistolary form is showcased through her ability to preserve Celie's and Nettie's intimate domestic viewpoints while also critiquing racial dynamics and integration. Walker's narrative strategies include employing a secondary narrative line for a post-colonial viewpoint and using kinship as a detailed metaphor for racial relations. These techniques allow her to highlight the personal stories of her characters while situating them within broader discussions of race and class.

Celie's initial struggle to interpret the envelope from Nettie might seem to reinforce the idea that her domestic viewpoint overlooks race and class issues. However, these lines not only highlights Celie's limited perspective but also introduces elements that encourage readers to reconsider her narrative within a broader context of race and class. While Celie sees only a "fat little queen of England" on the envelope, readers who recognize Queen Victoria can place this moment within a historical framework. The juxtaposition of British royalty with African imagery on the stamps, which Celie interprets as a sign of her ignorance, serves as a reminder of imperialism to more discerning readers. This marks Africa's first mention in the novel within a colonial context. Walker, skillfully maintains Celie's character authenticity while re-contextualizing her perspective. As Celie notices the stamps on the envelope, they carry political significance that might not be immediately apparent to her. The novel frequently embeds politically and historically charged elements like these, enriching the narrative with a post-colonial dimension and creating layers of thematic complexity. Just as *Huck Finn's* naïveté does not limit the social critique in Twain's work, Celie's limited awareness of the political implications in her letters does not diminish the novel's critique of race and class. This particular letter from Nettie exemplifies how the novel's domestic perspective is intricately marked by issues of race and class, illustrating the broader thematic concerns of Walker's epistolary approach.

The novel's exploration of race and class extends beyond mere narrative subtleties and shifts in context. Walker's portrayal of domestic life provides a profound examination of race through the nuanced depiction of family relationships, or kinship, serving as a recurring theme for understanding race relations. The novel challenges the separation between political and personal narratives by using family dynamics not only to present a vision of racial integration but also to examine that vision through the lens of integrated family structures in both Africa and America. Netties's letter to her sister said, "She says an African daisy and an English daisy are both flowers, but different kinds". The statement emphasizes that the theme of kinship, which is central to the narrative, becomes most pronounced towards the end of the novel, particularly during a scene where an adult Celie and a transformed Albert engage in communal sewing and conversation. It is in this moment that Celie directly addresses racial conflict by referencing the Olinka "Adam" story, a tale she has learned about from Nettie's letters. She starts by explaining that "... white people are black people's children" (231), the Olinka narrative provides an analysis of race relations expressed explicitly in terms of kinship. In the Olinka creation story, Adam is portrayed not as the first man but as the first white man born to an Olinka woman, cast out for his "colorlessness." This rejection led to a world of racial conflict, as the exiled descendants, enraged by their expulsion and perceived nakedness, resolved to oppress others, akin to crushing a snake. This narrative presents a counterpoint to the Judeo-Christian tale of Adam, redefining Original Sin not as the quest for knowledge or defiance of authority, but as the violation of kinship bonds. "What they did, these Olinka peoples, was throw out they own children, just cause they was a little different" (232). By recounting the Olinka narrative, Celie articulates complex thoughts about the social construction of racial inferiority. The myth presents this inferiority as a product of power dynamics that are subject to change over time. The Olinka anticipate that eventually, the whites will kill off so much of the earth and the colored that everybody gon hate them just like they hate us today. Then they will become the new serpent" (233). The Olinka creation narrative poses a key question central to the novel's broader theme: Can progress in race relations be achieved? Celie observes that some Olinka believe the cycle of discrimination will perpetuate indefinitely, suggesting that"…. life will go on and on like this forever," with first one race in the position of the oppressor and then the other. But others believe that progress in racial harmony is possible - that Original Sin may be alleviated - through a new valorization of kinship bonds:"... the only way to stop making somebody the serpent is for everybody to accept everybody else as a child of God, or one mother's children, no matter what they look like or how they act" (233). However, the universalist aspiration of this domestic ideal is tested by the novel's portrayal of historically situated, integrated kinship groupings in both Africa and America. Two significant examples are the relationship between white missionary Doris Baines and her black African grandchild in Africa, and the bond between Sophia and her white charge, Miss Eleanor Jane, in America. These integrated family units are used to expose and critique the broader patterns of racial integration within their respective contexts. When Nettie encounters Doris and her adopted grandson on a trip from Africa, seeking assistance for the displaced Olinka in England, she describes the scene as "incredible" due to the presence of this integrated family on board. The sight of an elderly white woman traveling with a young black child causes a stir among the ship's passengers, highlighting racial tensions as groups of white people fall silent when they pass by

(193). While Doris's relationship with the boy seems to align with the ideal of treating everyone as "one mother's children," her interactions initially appear more accepting compared to the overt racism from other whites who shun them. Doris even describes her time with the boy as the "happiest" years of her life (196) and appears more sympathetic to the African villagers than other missionaries, who aim to convert rather than appreciate their existing way of life (195).

However, Nettie's observations cast doubt on the authenticity of their "kinship." Although the boy seems fond of Doris and accustomed to her, he remains unusually reserved around her, displaying a "soberly observant speechlessness" (196). His openness with Adam and Olivia suggests that he feels more at ease with black Americans than with his white grandmother. This behavior prompts questions about the viability of kinship across racial lines, suggesting that kinship might develop more naturally within racial groups. The nature of Doris's honorary kinship with the Akwee villagers is also critically examined. Doris's decision to become a missionary was less about altruism and more about escaping the limitations of upper-class English society and a dull marriage prospect" milkfed" suitors, "each one more boring than the last" (194). Nettie, familiar with the plight of the displaced Olinka, finds Doris's aristocratic woes trivial and mocks her decision to pursue missionary work as a reaction to her ennui: "was getting ready for yet another tedious date" (194).

Doris's motivations also shape her interactions with the Akwee. Her approach to missionary work reflects an imperial mindset rather than genuine kinship. She uses her wealth to establish a seemingly reciprocal arrangement that, in reality, reinforces her power over the villagers: "Within a year everything as far as me and the heathen were concerned ran like clockwork. I told them right off that their souls were no concern of mine, that I wanted to write books and not be disturbed. For this pleasure I was prepared to pay. Rather handsomely" (195). Her relationship with the Akwee, characterized by paternalism and transactional exchanges, fails to meet the maternal ideal of racial relations depicted in Olinka myths. Her reference to the villagers as "heathen" and her belief in their fundamental difference from Europeans further highlight her inability to fully accept them as kin, revealing the limits of her integrationist stance. She says, "She thinks they are an entirely different species from what she calls Europeans.... She says an African daisy and an English daisy are both flowers, but totally different kinds" (115) Doris's claim of owning the village of Akwee underscores her view of racial integration as a form of colonial possession rather than genuine kinship "I am a very wealthy woman," says Doris, "and I own the village of Akwee" (196).

Stripped of the overt religious zeal and racism characteristic of other missionaries, Doris Baines's relationship with the Akwee villagers unveils the deeper patterns of self-interest and paternalism shaping race relations in Africa. Doris's interactions reveal a hierarchical dynamic where her benevolence masks a subtler form of imperial control. When Nettie first arrives in Africa, she is struck by the presence of numerous white people and the striking resemblance of Monrovia's presidential palace to the White House in America, which "looks like the American white house" (119). Nettie's observations extend to the socio-political landscape: whites hold prominent positions in the government, black cabinet members' wives emulate white fashion, and even the black president refers to his people as "natives"—a term Nettie notes with surprise, "It was the first time I'd heard a black man use that word"(120). Monrovia's Western influence is evident not only in its architecture but also in its socioeconomic practices. The city's cocoa plantations exemplify the colonial model of integration, with white individuals controlling economic activities from port towns to governor's mansions, "run by a white man" who rents out "some of the stalls .. . to Africans" (127). The displacement of the Olinka villagers by English road builders—central to the African sections of *The Color Purple*—mirrors this colonial pattern of integration and exploitation.

Nettie's immersion in the Olinka's domestic sphere provides her with a firsthand view of this colonial process, even as she and other black missionaries inadvertently contribute to it. Nettie's motivation for going to Africa contrasts with Doris's self-serving reasons; her intent is rooted in a genuine concern for her heritage, "people from whom [she] sprang" (111). Yet, she is trained by a missionary society driven by duty rather than genuine care for Africa, reflecting a broader imperialistic agenda by white people" who "didn't say a thing about caring about Africa, but only about duty" (115). This imperialistic perspective is evident in the English fascination with an appropriation of African material culture. Nettie describes the English obsession with artifacts from Africa. The English have been sending missionaries to Africa and India and China and God knows where all, for over a hundred years. And the things they have brought back! We spent a morning in one of their museums and it was packed with jewels, furniture, fur, carpets, swords, clothing, even tombs from all the countries they have been. From Africa they have thousands of vases, jars, masks, bowls, baskets, statues - and they are all so beautiful it is hard to imagine that the people who made them don't still exist. (116-17). The detailed inventory of these appropriated treasures underscores Walker's skillful blending of personal narrative with a critical examination of race and class. Nettie's awe at the artifacts symbolizes her initial wonder at her heritage but also serves to contextualize the broader implications of colonialism. Walker's narrative complexity is further highlighted through characters like Samuel and Corrine's Victorian aunts, Theodosia and Althea. The novel portrays these black women missionaries as remarkable figures who achieved significant accomplishments despite numerous challenges. The narrative encourages readers to admire their dedication and perseverance: "These very polite and proper young women, some of them never having set foot outside their own small country towns, except to come to the Seminary, thought nothing of packing up for India, Africa, the Orient. Or for Philadelphia or New York"(199). Through these nuanced portrayals, Walker maintains the integrity of the personal perspectives of her characters while critically engaging with the broader racial and imperial contexts.

In *The Color Purple*, Walker delivers her sharpest critique of missionary work not through the figure of Doris Baines but through Aunt Theodosia, particularly criticizing the misguided pride she takes in a medal awarded by King Leopold. This medal, given for "service as an exemplary missionary in the King's colony," becomes a symbol of Theodosia's unwitting complicity with Leopold's brutal regime, which decimated countless African lives, "unwitting complicity with this despot who worked to death and brutalized and eventually exterminated thousands and thousands of African peoples" (200). The narrative's critical edge is sharpened by the presence of a young "DuBoyce" at Aunt Theodosia's gathering. His commentary starkly exposes the medal as emblematic of the broader imperialistic exploitation carried out under the guise of missionary work. DuBoyce's intervention acts as a final, authoritative judgment on the entire missionary enterprise in Africa. Walker uses Nettie's letters to delve into the implications of missionary work, effectively achieving several objectives. First, these letters offer a credible and practical pathway for Nettie and other black missionaries to engage with the African domestic sphere. Second, they highlight the connections between philanthropy and colonialism, using Doris Baines's integrated family to critique the overarching missionary pattern of integration in Africa. Finally, Walker's embedded narrative allows her to remain faithful to her characters' perspectives while dissecting the racial and class hierarchies first introduced through Nettie's observations, such as the symbolic envelope from her sister.

Similarly, the relationship between Miss Sophia and her white charge, Miss Eleanor Jane, in the American South functions as a counterpoint to Doris Baines's situation, revealing the complexities of racial integration in a different context. Sophia, subjected to brutal treatment when she initially refuses to work for Miss Millie, is eventually coerced into becoming the mayor's maid, but she answers "hell no" (76). Her relationship with Miss Eleanor Jane, while seemingly affectionate, underscores the distorted dynamics of racial integration and the idealization of the black mammy figure. Miss Millie's request for Sophia to work as her maid comes after Sophia suffers a brutal beating by the mayor and six policemen, which leads to her imprisonment. While imprisoned, Sophia is subjected to harsh conditions, including forced labor in the jail's laundry, pushing her to the edge of sanity. In a desperate bid to escape prison, she agrees to become Miss Millie's maid. Sophia's confrontation with the white officers highlights the stark issues of race and class, which critics often point out are central to the novel. However, the critique extends beyond these dramatic public encounters. Sophia's complex domestic relationship with Miss Millie and the mayor's family offers a more nuanced examination of racial integration, a dimension that is frequently overlooked. Much like the bond between Doris Baines and her Black grandson, the relationship between Sophia and Miss Eleanor Jane seems to reflect genuine emotional ties amidst the broader racial and social constraints. Miss Eleanor Jane and is the one sympathetic person in her house, it is not surprising that the young girl "dote[s] on Sophia" and is "always stick[ing] up for her" (88), or that, when Sophia leaves the mayor's household (after fifteen years of service). Miss Eleanor Jane continues to seek out her approval and her help with the "mess back at the house" (174). Sophia's feelings for Miss Eleanor are, of course, more ambivalent. When she first joins the mayor's household, Sophia is completely indifferent to her charge, "wonder[ing] why she was ever bom" (88). After rejoining her own family, Sophia resents Miss Eleanor Jane's continuing intrusions into her family life and suggests that the only reason she helps the white girl is because she's "on parole. . . . Got to act nice" (174). But later, Sophia admits that she does feel "something" for Miss Eleanor Jane "because of all the people in your daddy's house, you showed me some human kindness" (225).

This perverse kinship exposes the unrealistic and harmful stereotypes of the black mammy figure. Sophia, who is more suited to roles outside of domestic service, is nevertheless forced into this position by societal expectations. Her struggle with Miss Eleanor Jane's unrealistic assumptions about her feelings and duties underscores the broader issues of race and class. The young Miss Eleanor Jane's expectations—that Sophia should naturally love and care for her as a maternal figure—reveal the disconnect between white perceptions and the realities of black lives (224-25). Through this complex portrayal, Walker critiques the myth of the black mammy and highlights the deeper issues within the racial dynamics of the American South. Historically, defenders of slavery employed the image of the black mammy to justify the institution, arguing that the plantation system was beneficial to enslaved individuals by integrating them into supposedly superior white families. This rhetoric suggested that slavery provided a framework in which enslaved people were cared for within the domestic sphere of white households. Sophia directly challenges this notion in *The Color Purple* by highlighting the absurdity of these claims. She criticizes the idea, "They have the nerve to try to make us think slavery fell through because of us. Like us didn't have sense enough to handle it. All the time breaking hoe handles and letting the mules loose in the wheat" (89). Sophia's experiences in the mayor's household further deconstruct this plantation model. Despite her supposed role as a subservient domestic figure, Sophia's interactions reveal the incompetence of her employers. For instance, Miss Millie, the mayor's wife, is portrayed as unable to drive effectively, even failing to complete a simple task like reversing the car. Miss Millie's inability to drive home alone underscores her reliance on Sophia, who must cut short a rare visit with her children to assist the flustered white woman. This situation exposes Miss Millie's dependence and highlights the fallacy of the supposed benevolent kinship promoted by plantation apologists. The narrative uses Sophia's domestic role to subvert the plantation discourse of kinship, suggesting that it not only perpetuates a false notion of family but also supports those who are inherently inept. As Sophia puts it, the plantation system's proponents view her and others as "backward, clumsy, and unlucky" (89), but it is the white characters who are shown to be incompetent.

In the American South, the model of integration based on the plantation system reveals a similarly deceptive kinship. Miss Eleanor Jane's husband's comments about the role of black mammies in raising children, while intended as a compliment, actually perpetuate a myth that ignores the complex reality of racial relationships. He says, "Everybody around here raised by colored," reflecting an idealized but superficial understanding of black women's roles (222). Simultaneously, white men in the South, such as the Sheriff in Celie's observation, maintain a denial of true familial connections with black women and their children. As Celie notes, Mr. 's son Bub "looks so much like the Sheriff, he and Mr. are almost on family terms," but this recognition only extends to acknowledging Bub's racial difference (76-77).

Actually, the fundamental system of kinship in the American South is more closely tied to the influence of white uncles than to the role of black mammies. This becomes evident in the scene where Sophia's family and friends discuss different strategies to secure her release from prison. "Who the warden's black kinfolks?" (80) Mr. reveals that kinship relations between whites and blacks are so extensive in the community that it may be assumed that someone will be related by blood to the warden. That someone, of course, is Squeak. Hopeful that she will be able to gain Sophia's release from the warden on the basis of their kinship, the others dress Squeak up "like she a white woman" with instructions to make the warden "see the Hodges in you" (82). In spite of the fact that the warden does recognize Squeak as kin "the minute [she] walk[s] through the door" (83) - or perhaps because he recognizes her - the warden rapes Squeak, denying their kinship in the very act of perverting it. As Squeak herself recounts, "He say if he was my uncle he wouldn't do it to me" (85). Both an intensely personal and highly political act, Squeak's rape exposes the denial of kinship at the heart of race relations in the South and underscores the individual and institutional power of whites to control the terms of kinship - and whatever power those definitions convey - for their own interests (13).

Sophia's rejection of Miss Eleanor Jane's baby is a deliberate act of resistance against the prevailing power structures and a challenge to the Olinka kinship ideals regarding race relations. From the moment her son is born, Miss Eleanor Jane persistently probes Sophia's maternal instincts toward the child. "shoving Reynolds Stanley Earl in her face" almost "every time Sofia tum[s] around" (223). When an exasperated Sophia finally admits that she doesn't love the baby, Miss Eleanor Jane accuses her of being "imnatural" and implies that Sophia should accept her son because he is "just a little baby!" (225). From Sophia's perspective as a persecuted Black woman, Reynolds Stanley is far from being just an innocent baby who should not be held accountable for the sins of his ancestors. While he may appear to be a "sweet, smart, cute, innocent little baby boy" to others, Sophia sees him as the grandson and namesake of the man who brutally assaulted her, a man whom Reynolds Stanley closely resembles.

Described as a "white something without much hair" and "big stuck open eyes" (223), Reynolds Stanley not only inherits his grandfather's physical traits but also benefits from the systemic privileges denied to Sophia's own children, who are sent off to fight in the military while Reynolds Stanley's father is excused to manage the family's cotton gin. To Sophia, Reynolds Stanley symbolizes the very system that oppresses her, representing the continuation of the societal structure that has wronged her. She questions, "He can't even walk and already he's in my house messing it up. Did I ask him to come? Do I care whether he's sweet or not? Will it make any difference in the way he grows up to treat me what I think?" (224). In doing so, Sophia challenges Miss Eleanor Jane's perception of Reynolds Stanley's "innocence" and asserts a strong opposition to the Olinka kinship ethic, which promotes treating everyone as if they are one's own children. ".. . all the colored folks talking bout loving everybody just ain't looked hard at what they thought they said" (226).

By challenging the plantation model of kinship and the stereotypical "mammy" role imposed on Black women, Sophia's position as an unwilling domestic in the mayor's household highlights the significance of personal perspectives in the novel's critique of race relations. In *The Color Purple*, this personal viewpoint is crucial to delivering its political commentary on racial injustice. It is precisely the African American woman's subjectivity that gives the lie to cultural attempts to reduce her – "like Sophia - to the role of the contented worker in a privileged white society" (14). Ultimately, Walker's portrayal exposes how Southern whites, like their historical predecessors, perpetuate a counterfeit notion of family and kinship. They cling to an idealized version of racial integration while systematically denying the genuine connections and responsibilities that exist between white and African American families. In *The Color Purple*, the narrative closes with a celebration of kinship and unity, encapsulated in a series of family reunions. Sophia and Harpo reconcile, Shug reconnects with her estranged children after thirty years, and the two narrators, Celie and Nettie, are joyfully reunited. Even Celie and Albert mend their relationship, which is signified by Albert's earning the right to be addressed by his first name. These reunions, occurring after Celie's journey to economic independence and emotional stability, underscore the vital role of kinship in achieving individual happiness.

As Nettie introduces her husband and children, Celie proudly identifies her own family: Shug and Albert o "point up at [her] peoples .. . Shug and Albert" (243). This moment highlights that an individual's full potential is realized within the supportive bonds of a strong kinship group, regardless of how unconventional that group may be. Additionally, the novel's conclusion engages with racial progress, as suggested by the Olinka Adam narrative. By resolving two key plot threads—

Sophia's interactions with Miss Eleanor Jane and her changing relationship with work—the story suggests that progress in race relations is indeed possible. However, the narrative also presents striking images of racial segregation in both Africa and America, complicating the notion of progress and pointing towards a nuanced understanding of kinship based on race. Sophia and Miss Eleanor Jane's reconciliation comes after Miss Eleanor Jane learns the truth about why Sophia initially worked for her family. Miss Eleanor Jane begins to assist Sophia in her home, indicating a shift in their relationship. When questioned by her family about working for African Americans, Miss Eleanor Jane retorts, "Whoever heard of somebody like Sophia working for trash?" Sophia's acceptance of Miss Eleanor Jane into her home signifies progress, even though Sophia sidesteps her feelings about Reynolds Stanley, Miss Eleanor Jane's child, by stating, "Henrietta say she don't mind him" (238). This response acknowledges Sophia's complex emotions while leaving open the possibility of change in future generations.

Sophia's employment at Celie's dry goods store further symbolizes a shift in race relations. It marks Sophia's escape from her role as a mammy and signifies economic and social integration between blacks and whites. The novel contrasts Celie's real father's successful store ownership, which was destroyed by white competitors unwilling to tolerate free competition, with the hardships faced by African Americans in accessing the "American Dream." This history forces a re-evaluation of Celie's family's past and highlights the broader systemic barriers that African Americans faced in achieving economic success. Through these complex layers, *The Color Purple* illustrates the ongoing struggle for racial equality and the importance of kinship in overcoming these challenges. Alphonso, Celie's stepfather, contrasts his approach to economic integration with that of Celie's real father by emphasizing a strategy of appeasement and manipulation. Believing that Celie's real Pa Didn't know how to git along," Alphonso, her step-pa, expresses a different path to economic integration: "Take me, he say, I know how they is. The key to all of 'em is money. The trouble with our people is as soon as they got out of slavery they didn't want to give the white man nothing else. But the fact is, you got to give 'em something. Either your money, your land, your woman or your ass. So what I did was just right off offer to give 'em money. Before I planted a seed, I made sure this one and that one knowed one seed out of three was planted for him. Before I ground a grain of wheat, the same thing. And when I opened up your daddy's old store in town, I bought me my own white boy to run it. And what make it so good, he say, I bought him with whitefolks' money. (155).

Alphonso boasts about paying off whites and even employing a white boy to run the dry goods store, using white people's money to do so. This behavior aligns him with the tradition of the trickster, manipulating the system for personal gain. However, this model of integration is ultimately accommodationist, as Alphonso closely associates himself with white power structures. From the beginning, he is depicted alongside armed white men, and his wealth leads him to adopt a lifestyle and domestic arrangements that mimic white paternalism. His marriage to a very young girl, whose family works for him and lives on his land, further exemplifies his internalization of these power dynamics. Shug asks Alphonso's new wife, a "child" not "more than fifteen," why her parents allowed her to marry him, the girl replies: "They work for him. . . . Live on his land" (154). Alphonso's marriage thus makes explicit the degree to which his identification with white paternalism shapes his domestic relationships with other blacks. Sophia's employment in Celie's dry goods store represents a significant departure from this history of compromise and exploitation. For the first time, the store features an integrated workforce, as Celie retains the "white man" working there while hiring Sophia to serve black customers. Unlike the oppressive white clerk who once intimidated Corrine, Sophia does not pressure customers and instead excels at sales by not caring whether they buy anything, "she don't care if you buy or not.". She also resists the imposition of plantation kinship roles, humorously challenging a white clerk who calls her "auntie" by asking which Black man his mother's sister married. Although the store's environment is not without its racial tensions, Sophia's role there marks both a personal victory for her and a communal success for the Black community. It signifies a shift towards greater respect and autonomy for African Americans in the marketplace, challenging the subservient roles they were historically forced into.

The Color Purple suggests that progress in race relations comes not from achieving the Olinka ideal of treating everyone as "one mother's children," but from a growing sense of racial identity and separatism within African and African American communities. By the novel's end, the possibility of universal kinship is realized within racial groups rather than between them. This is illustrated through the emergence of Pan-Africanism in Africa and the beginnings of Black Nationalism in the American South. In Africa, this separatism is embodied by the mbeles, a group of warriors who resist white rule and refuse to work for whites. Composed of individuals from various African tribes, "from dozens of African tribes," the mbeles are not defined by traditional bloodlines but by their shared experiences of racial oppression and commitment to resistance. Their actions, aimed at the removal of white colonizers, "missions of sabotage against the white plantations" (234) reflect a nascent pan-Africanism, with members even including a "colored man" from Alabama, highlighting a kinship based on racial identity rather than nationality.

While *The Color Purple* suggests that racial identity can surpass national boundaries, it offers no similar hope that racial divides can be easily bridged. This reality is underscored by two contrasting attempts at integration. Shug's son, a missionary on an American Indian reservation in the West, fails to be accepted by the indigenous community, who, as Shug explains, are dismissive of anyone who is not Native American ("everybody not an Indian they got no use for") (237). This stands in stark contrast to Mary Agnes's successful integration with the diverse communities in Cuba. Her acceptance there highlights how racial identity remains pivotal to kinship. Although some Cubans are as light-skinned as Mary Agnes and others are much darker, they are all considered part of the same family because of their shared racial identity. Shug notes that trying to pass as white is futile, as someone's heritage inevitably comes to light ("Try to pass for white, somebody mention your grandma") (211). Ultimately, the novel demonstrates that, whether in Cuba, Africa, or North America, racial identity among marginalized groups shapes and reinforces kinship connections. Walker, while developing her domestic metaphor for race relations, effectively highlights the personal experiences of her narrators and simultaneously offers a nuanced critique of racial integration. Walker's portrayal of integrated families underscores that the Black family has rarely existed as a private, middle-class entity insulated from state interference; instead, the African American household is deeply embedded with social meanings ripe for exploration. Rather than drawing a stark line between public and private realms, Walker's narrative emphasizes their interconnectedness. If there is an opposition in the narrative, it is not between public and private discourses, but rather between the universalist ideals of the Olinka perspective on race relations and the historical experiences of African Americans as depicted through specific integrated family structures. The Olinka ideal challenges the nature of kinship within these families, while the families themselves critique the Olinka myth for attributing racial discrimination to an imagined flaw in Black people, rather than acknowledging the real, historical discrimination imposed by whites. The novel's conclusion, which hints at a growing sense of racial separatism, does not necessarily conflict with the Olinka ideal. It may be that addressing past discrimination requires first dismantling false notions of kinship and discovering a shared sense of family among the marginalized, as a precursor to recognizing everyone as part of the same human family. Like the Olinka myth, the ending of Walker's novel poses questions about the future of race relations but offers no definitive answers. Critics argue that *The Color Purple* sacrifices its critique of the public sphere in favor of exploring personal experiences risk oversimplifying the narrative's complexity and missing its ongoing critique of racial integration from within the domestic sphere. Through its intricate narrative structure and detailed kinship metaphor, the novel probes the possibility of treating everyone as "one mother's children" while remaining acutely aware of the gap between noble ideals and historical realities.

52

Works Cited

Berlant, Lauren. "Race, Gender, and Nation in *The Color Purple*." *Critical Inquiry*, vol. 14, no. 4, 1988, pp. 831–859.

Butler-Evans, Elliott. *Race, Gender, and Desire: Narrative Strategies in the Fiction of Toni Cade Bambara, Toni Morrison, and Alice Walker*. Temple University Press, 1989.

Hooks, Bell. "Writing the Subject: Reading *The Color Purple*." *Alice Walker: Critical Perspectives Past and Present*, edited by Henry Louis Gates Jr. and K. A. Appiah, Amistad, 1993, pp. 460–467.

Stade, George. "The Color Purple: An Existential Novel." *The New York Times Book Review*, 25 April 1982, pp. 13, 26.

Walker, Alice. *The Color Purple*. Harcourt, 1982.

Chapter – 4
Violence of Language

Language is a powerful communication medium, enabling individuals to express their thoughts and engage with others. It fosters relationships of exchange, creating connections and bonds among its users. "As a multifaceted tool, language is a force for social cohesion, bringing people together through shared understanding (Sîrghi 81)". To speak is to make one's inner world audible, to communicate and engage in dialogue. However, language can also be a vehicle for violence, particularly when its influence—whether harmful or otherwise—affects the person it is directed towards. In this context, violence is understood metaphorically as the damaging impact that language can have on the recipient. "When wielded with harmful intent, language becomes an oppressive force, capable of inflicting psychological and moral destruction (Ricœur 32)". In such instances, the victim is subjected to a process of internal breakdown, often without the capacity to resist or escape. "Language is never neutral; it always carries an underlying intention or desire. In gendered interactions, especially between men and women, language often reflects and reinforces power dynamics, with men seeking dominance over women (Collins 125-26)". This struggle for control through language is vividly portrayed in Alice Walker's *The*

Color Purple, where the narrative intricately weaves instances of linguistic violence.

This chapter examines how language functions as both a tool of subjugation and a means of victimization. It explores how individuals are gradually confined within a discursive framework that limits their agency, leading to moral and psychological fragmentation. At the same time, language is a form of catharsis—a means for the oppressed to become aware of their condition and, in turn, take action to change it. This transformative form of violence, which I term positive violence, reframes the concept of violence from a symbol of oppression to a vehicle for self-awareness and liberation. At the beginning of *The Color Purple*, Alice Walker writes: "You better not never tell nobody but God. It'd kill your mammy." Although the sentence may seem to offer advice, it is, in reality, a warning and a subtle threat to Celie, the story's protagonist. It encapsulates what I describe as the "violence of language," which is central theme of this chapter. Through this concept of linguistic violence, I aim to explore the various ways in which language affects the lives of the characters—particularly the female ones—and subjects them to harm. By telling Celie not to share her experience with anyone except God, the speaker not only advises her but also warns her of the potential consequences: that her mother might suffer a heart attack or a moral shock severe enough to lead to her death. While death is an inevitable part of the human experience, it elicits both fear and trauma. Celie is acutely aware that the loss of her mother would deeply affect her, and so, burdened with this knowledge, she silently endures her suffering. In this context, the violence of language manifests as an attempt to suppress the unspeakable reality of the physical and verbal abuse that Celie endures. The simplicity and style of Celie's language in *The Color Purple* vividly mirror her distressed and tumultuous emotional and psychological state. Walker describes Celie's language as an authentic reflection of her identity, writing, "She has not accepted an alien description of who she is; neither has she accepted completely an alien tongue to tell us about it. She is affirmed by the language in which she reveals and likes everything about her; it is characteristic, hard-won, and authentic." Walker's use of language for Celie is both deliberate and grounded in the Black Southern oral tradition. She explains that Celie's speech reveals an intelligence that elevates her seemingly illiterate speech into something both beautiful and powerful in conveying her worldview. Moreover, Celie's language reflects the impact of a racist and sexist system on her, and her development into a self-aware individual despite this oppression illustrates the persistent efforts by her oppressors to keep her subdued. Walker notes, "If and when Celie rises to her rightful, earned place in society, the world will be a different place" (Walker 133).

This chapter Violence and Language explores the complex relationship between language and violence, arguing that language itself can mediate and even perpetuate violence. This interconnection is crucial to understanding how language operates as both a tool of oppression and a source of suffering in Celie's life.

> Violence has its meaning in its other: language. And the same is true reciprocally. Speech, discussion, and rationality also draw their unity of meaning from the fact that they are an attempt to reduce violence. A violence that speaks is already a violence trying to be right: it is a violence that places itself in the orbit of reason and that already is beginning to negate itself as violence. (33)

When applied to the novel *The Color Purple*, the above citation helps illuminate the reality of the characters' interactions, revealing how most of the female characters are placed in positions of subjugation and degradation. In this context, violence is not merely about physical harm but, as Ricœur suggests, as a desire to dominate, the attempt to deprive the other of freedom or of expression; it is racism and imperialism (32). This dynamic parallels forms of racism and imperialism, not as overt political or territorial conquests, but as a broader system of categorization, victimization, and pervasive domination that overwhelms Black women. The violence in *The Color Purple* extends beyond a simplistic understanding of racism or imperialism. It is not solely about the resentment or ideological hatred that some groups may feel toward others, nor is it about the traditional sense of political, economic, and cultural subjugation that leads to alienation. Rather, racism and imperialism here reflect a systemic effort to silence and control, to strip individuals—particularly women—of their agency and ability to express themselves. This is where Ricœur's insight becomes particularly relevant: the oppressive attitudes of the male characters in the novel reflect a deliberate effort to negate the Black woman's freedom of speech and expression.

Through this lens, the male characters' actions in the novel serve as a metaphor for the broader cultural forces of patriarchy. By denying women the ability to think and act independently, these men enforce conformity to the patriarchal norms that govern their lives. The female characters, especially Celie, are not only subjected to physical and psychological abuse but also to a silencing that prevents them from claiming their voices and asserting their autonomy. A crucial aspect of this male domination is reflected in the interactions between the male and female characters. Celie's experience, in particular, can be seen as a heavy burden she must bear—not only to protect her mother from harm but also to safeguard her own emotional and psychological stability. Her victimization is first expressed in her recognition and denunciation of her father's oppressive attitude toward her, a key moment that marks the beginning of her awareness of the injustice she faces.:

"He never had a kine word to say to me. Just say You gonna do what your mammy wouldn't." (1) Also, Pa's command to her during their sexual relation adds to her oppression: "You better shut up and git used to it." (2)The language Pa uses here underscores the violence he inflicts on Celie, not only physically but psychologically and morally. His words reveal a deep cynicism, as he views Celie merely as a sexual object, a possession to be used at his will. Much like a slave, Celie is forced to endure his assaults, which wound her both in body and spirit. In this way, Pa mirrors the dehumanizing practices of capitalist and patriarchal systems of slavery, which, while stripping individuals of their humanity, also sought to shape them into constructed subjects who served the needs of the dominant order. Pa reduces Celie to a state of nothingness, attempting to mold her identity according to the rigid patriarchal norms of his society. Under these conditions, as a subaltern and an "other," Celie is unable to construct an independent sense of self. Every aspect of her life is defined by a male-dominated culture, where Pa and the other male figures function as key enforcers of this societal framework.

Metaphorically, the social structure in Walker's novel can be compared to a musical orchestra, with the male characters as the conductors, setting the tempo. From their privileged positions, they demand that the female characters adhere to their rhythm through obedience and submission, threatening to crush them if they resist.

This continual pressure to conform helps maintain the stability of the patriarchal order. Walker's choice of this structure is deliberate, drawing attention to the plight of Black women while presenting Black men as predators or "wolves" in their interactions with them. Celie's suffering, particularly at the hands of cruel and abusive men, evokes sympathy, and this is undoubtedly one of Walker's main aims in her work. The brutality—both physical and verbal—exercised by the male characters is intended to subjugate the female characters, keeping them in a position of oppression and control, unable to escape the yoke of patriarchal dominance. When Shug Avery asks Harpo to help Celie with the household chores, his response highlights the deeply ingrained mindset of cultural supremacy. It reveals how men often use violence—not just physical, but also psychological and verbal—as a way to assert their dominance and enforce societal norms. In this exchange, men's need to demonstrate power and control often manifests as a form of violence that follows the discourse, shaping how relationships unfold and reinforcing patriarchal structures. The conversation between Shug and Harpo exemplifies this dynamic, where words and actions are used to navigate, maintain, and justify a system of inequality.

Time for you to help out some.

Women work, he say.

What? She say.

Women work. I'm a man.

You're a trifling nigger, she say. (22)

In this exchange, Harpo's refusal to help Celie does more than simply illustrate his resistance—it reflects a profound expression of male chauvinism that positions women as the sole caretakers of domestic labor. His repeated use of the phrase "women work" reinforces the cultural belief that domestic responsibilities are inherently female. Harpo's insistence that only women should carry out household chores reveals his attachment to phallic power. The violence in Harpo's words is not just in their content, but in how they widen the divide between him and Celie, reinforcing the gendered power dynamics of dominance and submission. By declaring that domestic work is women's responsibility, Harpo enforces a patriarchal hierarchy in which men occupy the superior role, while women are relegated to the subordinate, lower level. For Harpo, this gendered order must remain intact, as any shift would risk undermining his position of privilege within the family and community. Harpo's response, in this light, demonstrates how discourse functions as an expression of power. His words are a clear statement of his intentions and his claim to a specific position in the social order. Power, as a form of discourse, inherently involves struggle—one that is not defined by chaotic or uncontrollable forces but by positioning within a hierarchical system. By resisting Shug's request, Harpo challenges what he perceives as a reversal of patriarchal norms, advocating instead for the preservation of the traditional social order, which defines women's roles within the private sphere. Celie's passive inaction and her inability to express herself as an independent subject before Shug further serve to reinforce Harpo's quest for power. His desire for control over Celie is partly shaped by the way Black men, having been emasculated by the white-dominated society, seek to reassert themselves within their community through gender. Unable to confront the racial oppression that dehumanizes him, Harpo redirects his frustration toward gender relations, positioning himself as a man who can still maintain dominance over women within the family structure. In this way, his resistance to performing domestic work is not just a rejection of shared responsibility, but an assertion of lost masculinity and an effort to reclaim a sense of control within his household. Harpo's rhetoric of rejecting domestic labor serves as a way to reassert his patriarchal authority, pushing back against any perceived threat to the gendered status quo. This discourse is not just an expression of frustration, but an act of violence aimed at maintaining the hierarchy that grants him power and control. The violence here is not physical but linguistic—Harpo's words are a tool used to reinforce the boundaries of power and submission.

Celie's silence, on the other hand, exemplifies what sociolinguist Alexandra Sîrghi refers to as the "theory of the mute group," in her article "Insécurité linguistique des femmes dans l'espace public" (2011). According to Sîrghi, women in patriarchal societies are often deprived of their freedom of speech and expression, rendering them "mute" in the public sphere. In *The Color Purple*, this linguistic insecurity is not simply physical but emotional and psychological, manifesting in the ways women, especially Celie, are silenced and subjected to patriarchal expectations. Celie's letters, while they convey her suffering, are not expressions of self-empowerment; instead, they reflect her conditioning to conform to the social norms that demand her silence. Her language reveals not only her victimization but also her inability to challenge or control the linguistic codes that govern her interactions with men. As a member of the "mute group," Celie's silence is both a consequence of her oppression and a reflection of the patriarchal norms she must adhere to. Her passivity is a direct result of the gendered power dynamics that silence women, preventing them from speaking as independent subjects. Before Shug Avery enters her life, Celie remains trapped within this linguistic insecurity, unable to voice her desires or challenge the oppressive forces around her. The discourse of both Pa and Mr. ___ further emphasizes how language becomes a tool of domination in the hands of Black men, particularly as they exert control over Celie and other female characters. Pa is portrayed as a sexually violent figure who physically and psychologically abuses Celie, while Mr. ___ also embodies a more subtle form of sexism. Both men's language serves to silence Celie, preventing her from owning her "self" and asserting her autonomy. Their words, in line with Michel Foucault's ideas about power and discourse, in *The History of Sexuality* referred to by Bell Hooks in her article *"Reading and Resistance: The Color Purple"* that "discourse can be both an instrument and an effect of power" (Gates and Appiah, 1993: 284) highlight how language is used not just to communicate, but to enforce domination and suppress resistance. Through their brutal language, both Pa and Mr. ___ assert their control, reinforcing the patriarchal system that denies Celie the freedom to speak or define her own identity. When Celie tells Mr. ___ that she is planning to go North with Shug Avery, believing that she will find better opportunities and living conditions, his response is dismissive and mocking. He tells her that the North is not a place for people like her, revealing his deep-seated belief in racial and social hierarchies. His words are not just an attempt to discourage her, but also a way to reinforce the limitations placed on Celie as a Black woman. The underlying message in his statement is that someone of her status, race, and gender is not entitled to hope for a better life or to seek a place beyond the confines of the oppressive world she knows. In this moment, Mr. ___ uses language as a tool of control, dismissing Celie's agency and aspirations, while asserting the power of the societal structures that seek to keep her in her place.

You'll be back, he say. Nothing up North for nobody like you. Shug got talent, he say. She can sing. She got spunk, he say. She can talk to anybody.

Shug got looks, he say. She can stand up and be notice. But what you got?

You ugly. You skinny. You shape funny. You too scared to open your mouth to people. All you fit to do in Memphis is be Shug's maid.

her slop-jar and maybe cook her food. You not that good a cook either.

And this house ain't been clean good since my first wife died. And nobody crazy or backward enough to want to marry you, neither. What you gon do?

Hire yourself out to farm? He laugh. Maybe somebody let you work on they railroad. (212-13)

Mr. ___'s dismissive response to Celie's desire to go North is a clear example of how language can be wielded as a tool of negation and control. While his statement doesn't entirely align with Foucault's concept of language as power, it does underscore the role of language in undermining and limiting the autonomy of the female subject. His attempt to persuade Celie to abandon her dream of a better life in the North is not a rational argument but a calculated act of pressure—an attempt to silence her aspirations and reinforce her subjugation. Celie's dream of moving North can be read as symbolic of the historical migration of African

Americans, particularly the Great Migration when many Black Southerners fled to northern urban centers in search of better opportunities. However, they often encountered a harsh reality: unskilled labor, joblessness, and substandard living conditions. Mr. ___ seems to view Celie's desire as naive, dismissing her hopes with an almost bitter sense of cynicism. He tries to convince her that, as a Black, unskilled woman, she is destined to face the same disillusionment as many of those who sought a better life in the North only to find themselves trapped in poverty and exploitation.

Mr. ___'s approach, though grounded in a certain historical truth, is not simply one of discouragement but also one of control. His words serve to keep Celie within the constraints of her social position, reminding her of her supposed limitations and reinforcing the patriarchal order. In this sense, Walker's portrayal of Black men as both victims of racism and enforcers of patriarchal oppression adds depth to her critique of power dynamics within the Black community itself. While racism and White supremacy play a central role in the struggles of Black people, Walker suggests that internalized sexism and male chauvinism further entrench the suffering of Black women. This theme of language as a means of domination is also reflected in the epistolary form of *The Color Purple*. Celie's letters serve as a space for her to express her inner thoughts and feelings, a form of communication that allows her to reclaim some agency. In the beginning, Celie writes to God, expressing her deep suffering and longing for deliverance. These letters represent both her silence and her cry for help. The shift from letters to God, to her sister Nettie, to the broader world, and then back again to God, forms a circular narrative structure that reflects "Celie's evolving understanding of herself and her place in the world"(Walker 218). By the end of the novel, this cyclical movement toward God signifies her return to faith and hope, even as she begins to find her voice and assert her independence.

In *The Color Purple*, Walker's portrayal of language as a tool of violence not only illuminates the suffering of Black women but also the complexities of power within the Black community itself. Language becomes a way for characters to assert dominance, control, and subjugate others, particularly women, while also revealing the internalized oppression that shapes their lives. The novel suggests that true liberation for Celie, and other Black women, can only come when they find their voice, reject their victimization, and refuse to conform to the oppressive linguistic and social codes that have kept them silent.

An interesting point in Celie's letters is her language. The trial and error in her spelling at the beginning of the novel to find the correct grammar is very expressive: "I am fourteen years old. I am I have always been a good girl." (1) Celie's age—just fourteen—can be seen as a contributing factor to her early struggles with self-expression, particularly in her attempts to master grammar and language. It is common for young people of her age to still be in the process of acquiring language skills, and this is especially true for Celie, who has not had the opportunity for formal education. Her difficulty in finding the "right" words to express herself, and her frequent crossing out of what she has written, serve as a powerful metaphor for the silence and oppression she has endured. This act of trial and error in her writing is reminiscent of the experiences of enslaved people, who were prohibited from learning to read or write by their masters. The rationale behind this was clear: literacy fosters critical thinking, and education equips individuals with the power to question and resist authority. By keeping slaves illiterate, masters effectively stifled any potential for rebellion or self-determination. Celie's struggle with language, therefore, is not just about learning grammar; it echoes the deep historical legacy of forced illiteracy among enslaved African Americans. In the context of literature, many African American writers, including Alice Walker, use a mix of vernacular and Standard English as a way of reclaiming this history and perpetuating the voices of the oppressed. These linguistic choices highlight the enduring legacy of slavery while also demonstrating that, despite systemic barriers, enslaved individuals were able to communicate their experiences and resist their silencing. Celie's fragmented language and her grammar errors become a form of resistance, a way of speaking out despite the odds. Beyond the violence of negation, however, there is what I term "positive violence"—a type of force that does not inflict harm but rather acts as a transformative mechanism. This positive violence enables the individual to reassemble and empower their fragmented self within a hostile environment. In *The Color Purple*, this type of violence emerges in the relationship between Celie and Shug Avery. When they first meet, Celie is struck by Shug's self-assuredness, something she has lacked for so long. Shug, in turn, recognizes Celie's profound need for self-identity and individuality. Rather than simply pitying her, Shug takes a proactive role in helping Celie forge her personality, becoming a kind of surrogate mother or mentor. Shug's approach to Celie is one of emotional and psychological "violence" in the sense that she pushes Celie to confront and reshape her sense of self, even if it's uncomfortable or challenging.

A pivotal moment in this process occurs when Shug explains to Celie the nature of men's selfish desires for control, particularly in the context of gender dynamics. Shug's candid observations serve as a wake-up call for Celie, a moment of painful yet necessary growth. Through Shug's influence, Celie begins to realize that her suffering and passivity are not inherent to who she is, but are the products of a deeply entrenched patriarchal system. Shug's role in Celie's life is not just as a romantic or emotional figure, but as someone who disrupts the ingrained violence of silence and passivity. In this sense, Shug becomes a positive force in Celie's life—pushing her to confront her past, break free from the constraints of patriarchal subjugation, and embrace her true self.

Man corrupt everything, say Shug. He on your box of grits, in your head, and all over the radio. He try to make you think he everywhere. Soon as you think he everywhere, you think he God. But he ain't. Whenever you trying to pray, and man plop himself out on the other end of it, tell him to git lost, say Shug. Conjure up flowers, wind, water, a big rock. But this hard work, let me tell you. He been there so long, he don't want to budge. He threaten lightening, floods and earthquakes. Us fight, I hardly pray at all. Every time I conjure up a rock. I throw it. (204)

Shug's portrayal of men as social brutes—egoistic, oppressive figures—serves to highlight the deeply entrenched patriarchal power that dominates the world Celie inhabits. According to Shug, men wield power over everything around them, using their position to maintain control and prevent the flourishing of women. As the narrative expresses, "He been there for so long, he don't want to budge." This description emphasizes the stagnation of male dominance, with men so deeply entrenched in their privileged positions that they resist any change that might allow women to rise to their full potential. Shug's words are not just observations but serve as a call for Celie to recognize the limitations placed on her as a woman in a patriarchal society. Shug's discourse acts as a catalyst for Celie's awakening. She seeks to make Celie understand that she is living in a world that systematically denies her the freedom to possess her own identity. Through this "positive violence" of discourse—violence that forces an awakening rather than causing harm—Shug encourages Celie to realize that her selfhood has been stifled by the dominant social structures. The underlying message is clear: to regain her freedom, Celie must actively resist the patriarchal norms that oppress her. This insight, though painful, is the first step in Celie's journey toward self-empowerment. It is a form of violence that shakes her out of passivity, encouraging her to take the moral and psychological strength needed to envision and fight for a better future.

Shug's role in Celie's life mirrors the ancestral wisdom and mentorship that has long been a vital force in African American literature. As many scholars, including Toni Morrison, have pointed out, the figure of the older woman or maternal figure in African American women's writing is crucial for the emotional and intellectual development of the younger generation. These women, often portrayed as nurturers and guides, provide the emotional and psychological tools necessary for younger women to challenge their circumstances and find strength in their voices. Shug's guidance, in this sense, is not just personal empowerment for Celie, but also reflects a larger tradition of female solidarity and resilience in the face of oppressive systems. In this context, Shug's influence on Celie can be seen as a form of reawakening—a form of "positive violence" that serves as both a corrective and a transformative force. Shug pushes Celie to confront the harsh reality of her oppression, while also showing her that resistance and change are possible. It is through Shug's guidance that Celie begins to see that her suffering is not an inherent part of her being, but a product of patriarchal social norms. And it is through this realization that Celie starts to take control of her destiny, reclaiming her voice and her sense of self.

Ancestors are not just parents, they are sort of timeless people

whose relationships to the characters are benevolent, instructive, and protective and they provide certain kind of wisdom.

How the Black writer responds to that presence interests me. (Evans, 1984: 343)

Shug's role in Celie's life exemplifies the ancestral figure that Toni Morrison refers to in her analysis of African American literature. Throughout the novel, Shug takes on the role of a benevolent, guiding, and protective force for Celie, helping her navigate the painful reality of her subjugation. When Shug first meets Celie, she recognizes the depth of her trauma and emotional devastation. In response, she chooses to take Celie under her wing, not out of a desire for reciprocation, but out of a profound understanding that Celie needs help finding her strength. Shug's intentions are rooted in a deep care for Celie's well-being, and her sole request is that Celie becomes self-dependent, turning away from her past of silence and suffering. Shug's protective role is rooted in her desire to free Celie from the constraints of a patriarchal society that has long oppressed her. In their conversations, Shug teaches Celie about the nature of male power and its corrupting influence, explaining how men, through patriarchal systems, dominate everything in their sphere—including women. Shug's education of Celie is not merely intellectual but emotional and psychological. She provides Celie with the tools to understand the nature of her oppression, helping her see how male domination has shaped her identity and confined her sense of self. It is through Shug's guidance that Celie begins to recognize her worth and understand that she is capable of more than the victimhood that has defined her life until then.

In a broader sense, Shug's relationship with Celie also mirrors the traditional role that black mothers often play in the socialization of their daughters, as articulated by Wade-Gayles (1984). Black mothers, in many cases, are both nurturers and protectors, and they teach their daughters how to survive and thrive in a world that is hostile to them. Wade-Gayles discusses how these mothers impart survival strategies, not only for racial struggles but also for gender struggles, teaching their daughters how to assert their dignity and sense of self despite the oppressive forces they face. Shug embodies this maternal archetype for Celie, offering her wisdom and emotional support while helping her confront the harsh realities of her social and familial circumstances. Through Shug's mentorship, Celie gains the strength to imagine a life beyond her suffering. Shug not only helps Celie recognize her capacity for independence but also inspires her to question the patriarchal norms that have long governed her existence. By playing this role of maternal protector and guide, Shug empowers Celie to transcend her past victimization and start the journey toward self-empowerment and independence, ultimately allowing Celie to reclaim her voice and agency.

> Black mothers do not socialize their daughters to be 'passive' or 'irrational.' Quite the contrary, they socialize their daughters to be independent, strong, and self-dependent. Black mothers are suffocating, protective, and domineering precisely because they are determined persons in society who devalue Black women (Collins, 1991: 125-26).

The Color Purple presents characters that embody powerful transformations, particularly through Shug's role in Celie's life. Shug's relationship with Celie parallels the maternal bond, one where Shug, like a mother, imparts wisdom and prepares Celie to face the outside world—a world that has long confined her to silence and passivity. In this sense, Shug's guidance is rooted in personal experience, shaped by her survival and understanding of the oppressive forces around them. Much like a mother who teaches her daughter to navigate the dangers of the world, Shug instructs Celie to be wary of men and their patriarchal culture, which she views as the constant "enemy." This advice is not just a caution but a lesson in self-preservation and self-empowerment. Through Shug, Celie begins to understand the systems of power that have worked to silence and subjugate her. Shug embodies the timeless, ancestral role that Toni Morrison discusses, becoming a guardian figure who watches over Celie from the moment they meet, providing her the tools to resist the societal forces that have long oppressed her.

Shug's influence also reflects the complex and sometimes suffocating role of the mother figure, as described by Wade-Gayles. She expects Celie to break free from her passivity, to transcend the irrational fear and submission that have been instilled in her, and to become self-sufficient and strong. Shug's maternal care is not just nurturing, but also challenging. She pushes Celie to take responsibility for her survival, to assert herself, and to reclaim her dignity. Foucault's idea that discourse can function as both a hindrance and a point of resistance is particularly relevant here. Through Shug's words, Celie begins to understand that her silence, long viewed as a symbol of submission and powerlessness, can also serve as a form of resistance. The years of silence were not without purpose; they were a strategy of survival in a hostile world. However, as Shug encourages Celie to speak up, her silence is transformed into a powerful, self-affirming voice. No longer just a passive recipient of her fate, Celie gradually becomes an active agent in her own life.

This transformation is marked by Celie's increasing confidence, visibility, and self-assertion. Her voice—once suppressed—becomes a tool for her liberation. By the end of the narrative, Celie moves from being a helpless, unskilled, rural woman to a self-reliant and empowered individual. This shift is demonstrated when Celie writes about her time in Memphis with Shug, where she learns practical skills such as making pants, symbolizing her newfound independence and agency. Through Shug's mentorship, Celie evolves, overcoming the limitations imposed upon her by a patriarchal society. The narrative illustrates that, with the right guidance and encouragement, even those who have been silenced and marginalized can find their voice and reclaim their power. Celie's journey from silence to self-assertion echoes the larger struggle of oppressed groups, showing that the path to liberation often begins with an external force that helps awaken the dormant potential for resistance.

> I sit in the dining room making pants after pants. I got pants now in every color and size under the sun. Since us started making pants down home, I ain't been able to stop. I change the cloth, I change the print, I change the waist, I change the pocket. I change the hem, I change the fullness

of the leg. I make so many pants Shug tease me. (218).

Celie's evolving skills in making pants should not be interpreted merely as a sign of her initial unskilled state, but rather as a powerful manifestation of her desire for personal growth and perfection. For someone who has long lived in invisibility, Celie's efforts to improve her craft reflect her deep yearning to assert her individuality and demonstrate her capabilities. Each time she finds something unsatisfactory in the pants she is creating, she takes it upon herself to revise and perfect them, not simply out of necessity, but out of a desire to express her personality and create something of value. This attention to detail, and her insistence on improving her work, symbolizes her growing confidence and a deeper recognition of her potential. Her drive to perfect the pants is a metaphor for her larger journey toward self-actualization. Celie's previous years were marked by being silenced, subjugated, and dehumanized. Now, with the opportunity to create something tangible and valued, she pours her energy into perfecting her craft, not just to improve her product, but to carve out an identity for herself.

As the business expands and the demand for their pants grows, Celie's success becomes a turning point in her transformation. The creation of Folkspants Unlimited, a business venture that Celie and Shug embark on together, is not just an entrepreneurial success but a symbolic victory for Celie's autonomy and self-expression. By the time the business gets advertised in the local magazine, Celie is no longer the passive, invisible woman she once was. She is now a woman who has established her own identity, skills, and role in the world. This transformation is a testament to Shug's influence on Celie, and it echoes Shug's promise to help Celie become someone who can stand on her own. By bringing Celie to Memphis and encouraging her to explore her potential, Shug not only gives Celie a chance at independence but also provides her with the emotional and psychological space to rediscover herself. Shug's vow to help Celie emerge from her silence and passivity has been fulfilled. Celie is no longer defined by the oppressive forces that once controlled her but by her own will, creativity, and resilience.

In this way, Celie's development in making pants becomes a symbolic act of reclaiming agency. Through her hard work and perseverance, Celie achieves a sense of pride, individuality, and joy that was previously denied her. By perfecting her craft and building a business, Celie not only defines herself in the eyes of others but also in her own. This marks the culmination of her journey from a silenced, subjugated woman to a self-assured, empowered individual—proof of her determination to take control of her destiny. "I brought you here to […] help you get on your feet." In *The Color Purple*, Alice Walker delves deeply into the struggles of Black women, primarily through the character of

Celie, her central protagonist. This essay has explored two main aspects of the novel: first, how language can act as a tool of violence that subjugates and silences the individual, and second, how language can serve as a means of healing, providing comfort and self-empowerment to the fragmented subject. At the heart of this discussion is the Black woman, positioned as a marginalized and fragmented figure within a patriarchal society that imposes silence upon her and dictates her behavior. In such a society, any attempt by a woman to assert her individuality or personality is met with immediate resistance, as the rules and systems of power are designed to uphold the dominance of men.

Violence in Walker's novel is manifested in several forms, often taking on psychological and moral dimensions. For Celie, this violence begins with the oppressive words and actions of her father (Pa) and later her husband (Mr. __). Their treatment of her illustrates how language, specifically the words used by men, can be a form of violence that strips the individual of her autonomy, forcing her into a state of silence and submission. These men use language to reinforce patriarchal power, silencing Celie and leaving her fragmented both psychologically and emotionally. Their words embody the threat of violence, creating a stifling environment that denies Celie the freedom to express herself and claim her identity. Walker also presents a counterpoint to this violence through the character of Shug Avery. Shug's language, though initially tough and direct, serves a much more positive function. Rather than silencing Celie, Shug's words offer comfort, understanding, and guidance, helping Celie to reconstruct her fractured sense of self. Shug acts as a maternal figure who encourages Celie to embrace her own power, to confront the injustices of her past, and to rebuild her identity from the ashes of her trauma. Shug's role in Celie's transformation demonstrates how language can be a source of healing, offering the fragmented subject a means to resist, recover, and grow.

The key innovation in Walker's *The Color Purple* is the way the author addresses the Black experience from within the Black community itself. While Walker acknowledges the larger societal forces of racism and oppression, she shifts focus toward the internal dynamics within the Black community—particularly the ways in which Black men, struggling with their own marginalization, often perpetuate forms of violence and oppression within their own families. Walker does not shy away from critiquing Black men's roles in perpetuating patriarchal violence; instead, she invites a reflection on how these dynamics contribute to the broader system of gender and racial inequality. This introspective approach challenges the reader to understand that the Black community's problems are not only rooted in white supremacy but also in internalized gender hierarchies that affect both men and women.

In summary, Walker's portrayal of language as both a tool of violence and a means of healing provides a nuanced exploration of the Black woman's experience in a patriarchal, racist society. Through Celie's journey from silence and oppression to voice and empowerment, the novel underscores the complexities of Black womanhood and the transformative power of language. Whether as a tool of subjugation or a source of comfort and self-expression, language is central to the process by which Celie—and by extension, other Black women—navigates their oppression, finds their voice, and reclaims their agency in a world that seeks to silence them, , language is central to Celie's journey from oppression to empowerment (Foucault 78).

Works Cited

Collins, Patricia Hill. *Black Feminist Thought: Knowledge, Consciousness, and the Politics of Empowerment.* Routledge, 1991.

Evans, Mari. *Black Women Writers (1950-1980): A Critical Evaluation.* Doubleday, 1984.

Foucault, Michel. *The History of Sexuality, Volume 1: An Introduction.* Translated by Robert Hurley, Pantheon, 1978.

Gates, Henry Louis, and K. Anthony Appiah. *Alice Walker: Critical Perspectives Past and Present.* Amistad, 1993.

Ricœur, Paul. *Oneself as Another.* Translated by Kathleen Blamey, University of Chicago Press, 1992.

Sîrghi, Alexandra. "Insécurité linguistique des femmes dans l'espace public." *Langage et société*, vol. 137, no. 1, 2011, pp. 79–96.

Walker, Alice. *The Color Purple.* Harcourt, 1982.

Wade-Gayles, Gloria. *No Crystal Stair: Visions of Race and Gender in Black Women's Fiction.* Pilgrim Press, 1984.

Chapter – 5
Eco-Womanism in Alice Walker's Works: Intersections of Gender, Race, and Ecology

Alice Walker, in her exploration of womanism, presents it as a critical framework that uplifts and centers the experiences of Black women while advocating for a broader, more inclusive form of feminism. In her seminal work *Color Purple,* Walker defines a womanist as a Black feminist or feminist of color who not only values gender equality but also embraces racial, cultural, and familial heritage. Womanism, as opposed to mainstream feminism, acknowledges the unique struggles of Black women, who face both racial and gendered oppression. It highlights the interconnectedness of race, class, and gender, emphasizing the importance of community, spirituality, and creativity. Walker's concept of womanism encourages solidarity among women and men of color, fostering a vision of justice that is deeply rooted in love and holistic well-being. Through this perspective, she reshapes the feminist discourse, making it more inclusive and reflective of diverse lived experiences. Walker defined Womanism as follows:

A black feminist or feminist of color…

Appreciates and prefers women's culture, women's emotional flexibility (values tears as natural counterbalance of laughter), and women's strength…a womanist loves music. Loves dance.

Loves the moon. Loves the spirit.

Loves love and food and roundness.

Loves Struggle. Loves the folk. Loves her self.

(In Search of Our Mother's Garden: Womanist Prose 1983: XI, XII)

Alice Walker's work profoundly intertwines the experiences of women and the natural world, reflecting a deep empathy and concern for both. Her novels often spotlight the exploitation faced by women and environmental degradation. Notably, her Pulitzer Prize-winning novel *The Color Purple* (1982) exemplifies her approach to eco-womanism. This concept aligns with the definitions of "ecology" and "ecosystem," which highlight the interconnectedness of all living organisms and their environments on Earth. According to the Oxford Advanced Learner's Dictionary, "ecology" is defined as "… the relation of plants and living creatures to each other and their environment" ("Ecology," Def. 485). It defines 'Ecosystem' as "all plants and living creatures in a particular area considered with their physical environment" ("Ecosystem," Def.486). Both definitions underscore the interconnectedness between the living and non-living elements of our world. However, human activities have often disrupted this balance by altering ecosystems for personal gain. This has led to significant ecological imbalances that must be addressed to ensure a sustainable future for the planet. Additionally, the relationship between humans and the non-human elements of the environment has often been one-sided, with humans exerting dominance over both nature and women. In her novels, Walker addresses this imbalance by giving equal importance to men, women, animals, and the natural world, advocating for an eco-centric perspective through womanism. In *The Color Purple,* she connects environmental concerns with issues of gender and race, illustrating how these elements are interrelated. Ecocriticism examines issues such as environmental degradation, pollution, global warming, climate change, and species extinction, emphasizing the need for environmental awareness through literary representation. Scholars like Cheryl Glotfelty, Lawrence Buell, and Greg Garrard, in works such as The Ecocriticism Reader: Landmarks in Literary Ecology (1996), The Environmental Imagination: Thoreau, Nature Writing, and the Formation of American Culture (1995), and Ecocriticism (2004), have highlighted the ecological crises confronting modern society and proposed solutions like returning to nature and interdisciplinary studies of environmental issues. However, they have generally not addressed the link between the oppression of women and environmental degradation, a connection crucial for the liberation of both. The term 'Ecofeminism' first emerged in 1974 in Françoise d'Eaubonne's Le

Féminisme ou la Mort, where she discussed the direct relationship between the oppression of nature and women. It's often noted that "Sexism and exploitation of the environment are parallel forms of domination" (Warren i).

Spretnak aptly observes that

> Ecofeminism will address not only the interlinked dynamics in the patriarchal culture of terror of nature and the terror of elemental power of the female but also the ways of the mesmerizing conditioning that keeps women and men so cut off from our grounding in the natural world, so alienated from our larger sense of self (6).

Ecofeminists illustrate the interconnectedness of women's and environmental issues, yet they often do not integrate discussions of racism with gender and ecological concerns, a gap that eco-womanism addresses. Alice Walker introduced the term 'Womanism' in 1983 in her collection of essays, In Search of Our Mothers' Gardens: Womanist Prose, to address the unique struggles women of color face.

She defines a womanist as

> "A black feminist or feminist of color… who appreciates and values women's culture, emotional flexibility (seeing tears as a natural counterbalance to laughter), and strength." She

further describes a womanist as someone who "Loves music. Loves dance. Loves the moon. Loves the Spirit. Loves love and food and roundness. Loves struggle. Loves the Folk. Loves herself. Regardless" (Walker, In Search xi-xii). These definitions underscore that a love for nature is a core aspect of womanism.

Walker's body of work reflects her deep concern for both black women and the environment. Echoing the sentiments of ecofeminists like Spretnak, Walker advocates for 'ecological wisdom' to combat environmental degradation. She extends beyond traditional ecofeminism by integrating considerations of race with gender and promoting a perspective that challenges anthropocentric attitudes toward nature. As Smith notes, the term 'Ecofeminist' highlights the connection between environmental degradation and the oppression of women, racial minorities, and the marginalized. At the same time 'eco-womanist' emphasizes "how this perception uniquely impacts women of color" (476). Ecowomanism, therefore, is grounded in the lived experiences of African American women. Alice Walker redefines herself not just as an author but as a committed eco-womanist, engaging her readers through a composed and introspective exploration of humanity's detrimental impact on nature. She meticulously investigates and analyzes the pervasive threats imposed on the environment by human actions, emphasizing the urgent need for genuine eco-womanist consciousness to rectify the damages caused by environmental pollution, deforestation, and global warming.

In Walker's narrative, eco-womanism emerges as a powerful force capable of dismantling patriarchal hierarchies while simultaneously safeguarding the interests of women and the environment. Her works, notably *The Color Purple,* serve as poignant protests that resonate deeply with environmental concerns such as nurturing nature, combating deforestation, advocating for nuclear disarmament, and preserving nature-centered cultures. Walker portrays black women as historically rooted in a matriarchal culture deeply connected to nature—a culture that nurtured and protected their interests before their displacement to America. However, upon arrival, they were stripped of this understanding, and subjected to patriarchal dominance that alienated them from both their intrinsic nature and the natural world. This subjugation under patriarchal systems led to their stigmatization as pagans and witches, further exacerbated by patriarchal interpretations of Christianity that favored an anthropocentric worldview over an eco-centric one. Drawing on insights from scholars like Capra, Walker advocates for an eco-centric worldview that prioritizes the preservation of ecosystems for the benefit of women of color and all humanity. Her writings underscore the interconnectedness of racism, sexism, and environmental degradation, echoing her belief that "Earth itself has become the nigger of the world."

Through her literary contributions, Walker urges a spiritual reconnection between women and nature, rejecting patriarchal religiosity in favor of a more inclusive, eco-centric spirituality. This perspective, exemplified *in The Color Purple*, empowers female characters like Celie to reclaim their identities and find spiritual fulfillment through a profound communion with nature. "Every time I think I'm going to do something, I look at the sky, and I say, 'I know where I'm going to go.'" This line illustrates Celie's evolving sense of hope and direction, using the sky as a metaphor for her aspirations and dreams. For Celie, this journey signifies a transformative awakening, moving away from patriarchal constraints towards a harmonious existence within the natural order. "The trees are big and old and have a lot of secrets to tell. They have seen so much. I think about how they've grown, and how they've changed over time. I think about how I've grown and changed, too." This quote highlights how nature, symbolized by the trees, parallels the personal growth and transformation of the women in the novel, suggesting a deep, symbolic connection between them.

Thus, Alice Walker's work transcends mere storytelling; it serves as a rallying cry for ecological and feminist movements alike, advocating for a holistic worldview that cherishes both women and the environment as integral parts of a shared, interconnected universe. In the novel *The Color Purple*, Alice Walker emphasizes that addressing patriarchy alone is insufficient for the holistic liberation of women and the environment. Walker highlights how patriarchal forces erase cultural rituals and practices that celebrate female sexuality and pleasure. She argues that the liberation of female sexuality—while often stigmatized and repressed—can provide significant relief from the burdens imposed on women. Lovalerie King insightfully notes that Walker's portrayal of womanism is deeply connected to "Embracing one's fluid sexuality and expressing it freely in relationships" (King 138).

Walker's admiration for nature, as expressed in her work *Anything We Love Can Be Saved: A Writer's Activism* (1997), is reflected in *The Color Purple*. She draws parallels between the strength and resilience of nature and the struggles of her characters. Celie's identification with a tree symbolizes her enduring strength and capacity for growth despite her oppression. Shug, embodying ecological wisdom, nurtures and empowers other women, helping them achieve self-reliance. Celie's entrepreneurial success and the support of nature highlight Walker's belief that overcoming suffering involves removing internal and external toxins. In the lines, "I think about God, I think about nature. I think about how small and how big I am, and how much I want to see." Celie reflects on her place in the world, linking her personal growth to the vastness of nature and her desire to experience it. Later we see her conquering the world through her emancipation

Walker's pantheistic view of God, as expressed in an interview with John O'Brien, challenges traditional religious notions. She asserts that "the world is God, man is God, and so is a leaf or a snake" (O'Brien 75), rejecting the idea of a male, white God in favor of a more inclusive spiritual understanding. Shug's guidance helps Celie shift from a Christianity linked to white patriarchy to a pantheistic view, finding divinity in nature itself. This transformation reflects Celie's broader realization of the racial and gendered implications of Christian patriarchy. The novel illustrates that unity with nature is essential for personal and collective healing. Celie's newfound awareness is symbolized by her deep connection with nature—she finds solace in her farm and builds a home filled with natural artifacts, embodying her eco-womanist values. Shug's influence and Celie's growth highlight how eco-womanism fosters self-reliance and empowerment.

In *The Color Purple*, Nettie finds solace in nature during her time in Olinka, a village in Africa. As she adjusts to her new surroundings, she finds comfort and renewal in the natural beauty and rhythms of the land. The vibrant descriptions in her letters reflect her deep connection to the environment around her. "I wake up to the sound of birds and the sight of the sun rising over the horizon. It's a different rhythm from what I'm used to, but it's soothing."

This line captures Nettie's adaptation to her new environment and the comfort she finds in the natural rhythms of her surroundings. Nettie marvels at the fertile land and the lush vegetation of Olinka, which contrasts sharply with the barren landscapes she left behind. She writes about the "lush green plants" and the "scent of flowers," which provide her with a sensory escape from her loneliness and the hardships she faces. "The air is full of the scent of flowers. There is a tree with pink blossoms that I have never seen before. It makes me think of home, and how I miss you all." Here, Nettie's observation of the flowers and the tree ties her emotional state to the natural environment, reflecting how nature evokes memories and feelings. The natural world in Olinka, with its towering trees and rich flora, offers her a sense of peace and continuity, a balm for her spirit amid emotional upheaval.

Furthermore, Nettie observes the local people's harmonious relationship with nature. The way they farm the land with care and respect reinforces her sense of connection to the earth. This alignment with nature helps Nettie feel rooted and supported, as the land and its cycles become a metaphor for her healing and growth. "The land here is fertile and rich. The people farm it with great care and respect. The trees are strong and old, and they seem to hold stories of the past." Nettie's appreciation of the land's fertility and the ancient trees shows her respect for nature and how she perceives it as a keeper of history and culture. The rhythm of nature, the changing seasons, and the enduring beauty of her surroundings provide her with a renewed sense of hope and belonging, even as she remains separated from her family. "The land is very beautiful. I have seen so many animals that I never saw before. I have seen the monkey, the hippopotamus, and the giraffe. The way the land is, with the lush green plants and the mountains in the distance, makes me feel very close to God." This highlights Nettie's awe of the natural beauty in Africa and her sense of spiritual connection to the land.

Walker also uses Nettie's experiences in Olinka to underscore the impact of environmental degradation. The destruction of nature in Olinka mirrors global issues like pollution and deforestation, showing how these environmental crises are linked to broader patterns of exploitation (Bush 1039). Nettie's spiritual connection to nature aids her recovery and resilience against these challenges. "I've noticed the plants are not growing as they used to. The soil seems tired and less able to nourish the crops. The villagers are worried about the future, as the once fertile land is no longer yielding enough to sustain them." This reflects how environmental degradation is impacting agricultural productivity, leading to concerns about food security and the sustainability of the villagers' way of life. "I've noticed the plants are not growing as they used to. The soil seems tired and less able to nourish the crops. The villagers are worried about the future, as the once fertile land is no longer yielding enough to sustain them." This reflects how environmental degradation is impacting agricultural productivity, leading to concerns about food security and the sustainability of the villagers' way of life. Similar to the exploitation of women of color hampering the roots of survival of the black community.

The lesbian relationship between Celie and Shug is particularly noteworthy as it challenges male dominance and the violence faced by Black women. This relationship signifies a transformative step toward a more egalitarian society. Shug and Celie's embrace their sexuality, along with Sofia and Squeak's journeys toward self-discovery and reclaiming their sexual autonomy, further undermine patriarchal control and demonstrate how self-actualization can counteract male oppression. When Celie says, "Heaven, I know, is a beautiful place, for I have felt its breeze and seen its light." Celie's perception of heaven as a beautiful place tied to sensory experiences of nature highlights her deep connection with the natural world and her inner life. Walker's novel also illustrates the importance of reclaiming one's body and spirit. Through Celie's transformation with Shug's guidance and the self-discovery journeys of Sofia and Squeak, the characters reclaim their bodies and voices, overcoming abuse and asserting their identities. This revitalization aligns with Walker's broader theme that a harmonious relationship with nature and a reclamation of cultural and personal identity are vital for overcoming oppression. The novel underscores that the preservation of matriarchal traditions can effectively counteract patriarchal dominance and protect women's and environmental interests. Through the introduction of blues music, which reflects both the pain and resilience of the Black community, the characters find solace and empowerment. Sherley Ann Williams's observation on the blues—their capacity to express both suffering and triumph—resonates with the novel's depiction of how these songs help characters reconnect with their true selves and combat the impacts of racism, sexism, and classism (Williams 144). Walker's portrayal of this emotional connection underscores how art, culture, and nature collectively contribute to personal and communal healing.

Alice Walker advocates for women to challenge patriarchal power by dismantling the hierarchies upheld by organized religion and cultural practices that subordinate women and the environment to male interests. Walker posits that "all of creation is of the same substance and therefore deserving ... same respect," emphasizing that humans are as intimately connected to animals and nature as they are to each other (Walker, The Universe Responds, 307-308). This perspective critiques anthropocentric views that place humanity above nature. Instead, Walker endorses a cyclic connectivity among all elements of the world. Walker's concept of womanism incorporates an ecological perspective, valuing both animate and inanimate aspects of nature. She describes a womanist as someone who "loves music, dance, the moon, the Spirit, love, food, roundness, struggle, the Folk, and herself" (Walker, In Search xii), highlighting an integrated view of nature and spirituality. This eco-womanist approach is evident in the novel through the healing circles formed by the female characters, symbolizing unity and mutual support.

The reversal of traditional gender roles at the novel's end—between Celie and Albert, and Sofia and Harpo—reflects the dismantling of patriarchal hierarchies, leading to improved relationships between men and women and between Black and white characters. This shift supports the preservation of both women's and nature's interests. The novel concludes with Celie's address to the natural world in her final letter: "Dear God, Dear Stars, dear trees, dear sky, dear peoples. Dear everything..." (Walker, The Color Purple 292). This closing reflects her full embrace of Eco womanist awareness, culminating in her fulfillment and alignment with nature. Through *The Color Purple*, Walker emphasizes that a deep connection with nature is a manifestation of the female spirit and crucial for realizing true potential. The characters' journey toward eco-womanism illustrates how overcoming past oppressions and embracing environmental stewardship can lead to profound personal and collective empowerment.

Works Cited

Bush, Harold K. *The Ecology of Black Literature: Writing, Nature, and African American Intellectual Life*. University of Illinois Press, 2021.

Glotfelty, Cheryl, and Harold Fromm, editors. *The Ecocriticism Reader: Landmarks in Literary Ecology*. University of Georgia Press, 1996.

Garrard, Greg. *Ecocriticism*. 2nd ed., Routledge, 2012.

King, Lovalerie. *The Cambridge Introduction to Zora Neale Hurston*. Cambridge University Press, 2008.

O'Brien, John. *Interviews with Black Writers*. Liveright, 1973.

Spretnak, Charlene. *The Spiritual Dimension of Green Politics*. Bear & Co., 1986.

Walker, Alice. *The Color Purple*. Harcourt, 1982.

Chapter- 6
The Dawn of Independence

Alice Walker's novel *The Color Purple* is an epistolary tale centered on Celie, a poor Black woman living in a rural Georgia community near Eatonton, the author's birthplace. This acclaimed work was later adapted into a film produced by Quincy Jones and directed by Steven Spielberg. A parade in Walker's honor marked the film's premiere in Eatonton, and her sister Ruth established The Color Purple Foundation to support educational initiatives. In this chapter, we explore Celie's journey toward self-liberation, facilitated through her letters and the support of key women in her life. The novel emphasizes the powerful role of sisterhood in Celie's transformation, showcasing how her relationships with her sister Nettie, close friend Shug, and stepdaughter Sofia provide her with physical, spiritual, and emotional strength to overcome male oppression. Writing letters serves as a vital therapeutic tool for Celie, allowing her to process her suffering and move toward personal freedom. This chapter highlights how sisterhood and writing are crucial to Celie's path to emancipation.

The novel *The Color Purple* is widely regarded as one of the most impactful literary works highlighting the struggles of African American women against patriarchy, sexism, and racism. Alice Walker's goal extends beyond merely depicting these challenges; her true intent is to give a voice to Black women and offer a path to their liberation. Through the character of Celie, Walker illustrates a profound journey from a sexually abused child and passive wife to an empowered and emancipated woman. Walker expresses a deep admiration for Black women, stating, "For me, black women are the most fascinating creations in the world" (Walker 251). She aims to explore the dynamics between men and women and, more specifically, the experiences of Black women. Walker portrays the severe oppression Black women face in their interactions with Black men and underscores the critical role of sisterhood in their liberation. The transformative power of sisterhood in Celie's journey to freedom examines how female bonds contribute to Celie's physical, spiritual, and economic independence, and analyzes the significance of writing in her process of emancipation. Walker is deeply concerned with the "spiritual survival, the survival whole" of her community, noting that "black women among all women have been oppressed almost beyond recognition — oppressed by everyone" (Walker 149). Her compassion extends to those who have endured sexual exploitation and abuse, often labeled as "Matriarchs," "Super-women," or "Mean and Evil Bitches." Mary Helen Washington provides further insight to the novel:

> From whatever vantage point one investigates
> the work of Alice Walker — poet, novelist,

short story writer, critic, essayist, and apologist for black women — it is clear that the special identifying mark of her writing is her concern for the lives of black women." (Washington 133)

Celie's decision to write is partly a defiant response to her father's demand that she confide only in God about the abuse he inflicted on her, an act of control that seeks to strip her of both her voice and her children. Her writing thus becomes an act of rebellion against her abuser's attempts to silence her. Deborah McDowell highlights that the epistolary format not only underscores Celie's isolation and desperation but also affirms her independent voice (McDowell 1987: pp. 281-302). Through her letters, Celie finds a refuge from a patriarchal world that initially stifles her ability to express her struggles. These letters break the imposed silence and symbolize her deeper desire for freedom and self-expression. Celie's choice to write also reflects her lack of confidence in discussing her suffering with others. With her mother deceased, her school teacher unable to assist after her withdrawal from school, her sister fleeing to escape abuse, and her sister-in-law's efforts to challenge her oppressive environment thwarted by threats from her brother, Celie feels increasingly abandoned. This marginalization leaves her with only her faith in God until Sofia (her daughter-in-law) and Shug (her husband's mistress) enter her life, offering support and companionship.

It's important to recognize that Celie endures a period of solitude after her sister departs and before she encounters Sofia and Shug. During this challenging time, she lacks confidence, mentorship, and companionship, finding solace only in her pen and paper. Writing becomes her lifeline, a way to externalize her suffering and confront her inner demons. Through this act, she manages to persevere. Initially, Celie's letters are addressed to God, an abstract recipient, and later to her sister Nettie, who does not respond. This reveals that the primary function of the letters is for Celie's benefit rather than for any intended reader. Her writing is driven by desperation and a need to preserve her sense of self. In her letters, she seeks to alleviate her pain and find hope, a sentiment evident in the following lines:

> I have written to stay alive… I've written to survive", "writing poetry is my way of celebrating with the world that has not committed suicide the evening before." (McConkey 212) In this connection, McDowell points out : "Celie still had an attempt to affirm herself in the act of writing. Everything we learn about Celie is filtered through her own consciousness and rendered in her own voice." (McDowell Pp. 281- 302)

Celie's writing serves as a profound reflection of her inner self. As she writes from the heart, her style evolves, becoming increasingly refined, defined, and fluid. What begins as an intensely private and somewhat disjointed expression transforms into a more personal and coherent narrative that incorporates the lives of those around her. Through her letters, Celie creates a tangible representation of her experiences. These letters, which vividly document her suffering, become a means for her to confront and make sense of her pain. This practice helps her maintain her mental stability and prevents her from descending into madness. When Celie's husband intercepts Nettie's letters, she remains cut off from her sister for years. However, when Shug discovers and reads these letters aloud to Celie, it feels as though a new chapter of her life begins. Despite Nettie's physical absence, her moral presence is powerfully felt through the letters.

The materiality of Nettie's letters is significant for Celie. She introduces the recovered letters with personal references, such as, "This letter I bee holding in my hand" (TCP 112) and "the first letter say" (TCP 119). Beyond their physical significance, these letters contain crucial information about their past, including revelations about their real father's death and the true identity of 'Pa' as their stepfather. This new understanding profoundly affects Celie's psyche. She has been instructed to share her feelings only with God, as reflected in the text: "You better not never tell nobody but God. It'd kill your mammy" (Washington 133). Toni Morrison offers insights into the creative process, explaining that a writer must draw on personal memory to fuel their imagination. Over her extensive career, Morrison has emphasized that creative work is deeply rooted in the writer's own experiences and memories, "the process by which the recollections of these pieces coalesce into a part (and knowing the differences between a piece and a part) is 'creation'". (McConkey 212)

In the novel, men frequently struggle to understand the bonds between women. Samuel, for instance, finds the women of Olinka perplexing: "Because to him, since the women [of Olinka] are friends and will do anything for one another... Because the women share a husband but the husband does not share their friendship, it makes Samuel uneasy. It is confusing" (TCP 141). This highlights the idea that sisterhood is a unique and deeply personal connection that men often fail to grasp. The novel showcases numerous examples of sisterhood that forge strong connections among women. Celie and Nettie, living in a family devoid of affection, find solace in each other. Despite their violent, rapist father and ailing mother, Nettie offers Celie moral support. When Nettie learns of Celie's suffering at the hands of her husband, she encourages her to stand up for herself and assert her strength, even advising her to challenge Mr.____'s children to demonstrate her authority (TCP 25).

Sofia Butler, Celie's daughter-in-law, also serves as a significant role model. Raised in a male-dominated environment, Sofia learned early on that survival required resistance: "All my life I had to fight. I had to fight my daddy. I had to fight my brothers; I had to fight my cousins and my uncles. A girl child ain't safe in a family of men" (TCP 38). In contrast, Celie initially remains passive, accepting male dominance as a given. However, Sofia's defiance against societal norms and her refusal to be subdued by anyone, regardless of race, stand as powerful examples of resistance and empowerment. Celie's initial encounter with Sofia occurs when Sofia seeks Albert's permission to marry Harpo. Celie is struck by Sofia's commanding presence: "She's not quite as tall as Harpo but much bigger, and strong and ruddy-looking, like her mama brought her up on pork" (TCP 30). This first impression highlights Sofia's physical and emotional strength. Sofia later demonstrates her resistance to white oppression by rejecting an offer from the Mayor's wife to become a maid—a role historically imposed on Black women. Sofia's refusal is emphatic: "Hell no" (TCP 90). When the Mayor retaliates by striking her, Sofia defiantly fights back, knocking him down. This act of resistance is significant, as it challenges both racial and gender-based oppression. For Celie, Sofia's actions serve as a powerful lesson in standing up against all forms of oppression to preserve one's individuality and dignity.

When Albert insults Sofia about her pregnancy and rejects their request, Celie is amazed when Sofia refuses to submit. Sofia tells Harpo, "Naw, Harpo stay here.

When you free, me and the baby be waiting" (TCP 38). Sofia's courage deeply influences Celie. Despite societal objections, Sofia marries Harpo, and initially, they share a harmonious life. "They share the housework and enjoy their familial happiness. She makes some sheets, he takes the baby, gives it a kiss, chucks it under the chin" (TCP 33). Sofia maintains her independence, continuing to assert herself even in the presence of Harpo and Mr.____: "If she was talking when Harpo and Mr.____ came in the room, she keeps right on. If they ask for something, she says she doesn't know. Keeps talking" (TCP 34). However, this unconventional relationship clashes with the male-dominated societal norms. Albert's inability to tolerate Sofia's assertiveness leads him to incite Harpo to beat her. Celie, who has endured her suffering and is unaware of her oppression, even suggests that Harpo should follow through. When Sofia discovers this, she feels deeply betrayed. She confronts Celie, asking why she would act this way, to which Celie responds, "I say I'm a fool, I say it because I'm jealous of you. I say it because you do what I can't" (TCP 38). This exchange reveals Celie's admiration for Sofia's rebellious spirit. After Sofia learns that Celie has been confiding her suffering only to God, she advises Celie to take direct action: "to bash Mr.____'s head open, think about heaven later" (TCP 39). This honest conversation helps clear up misunderstandings and strengthens their bond, as shared experiences draw them closer. From that point on, Celie and Sofia develop a supportive friendship that helps both women navigate their challenges. Sofia's example teaches Celie about independence, strength, and courage, transforming Celie's self-perception and paving the way for her liberation. Similarly, Shug Avery plays a crucial role in Celie's journey to freedom, but their relationship is distinct from those with Nettie or Sofia. Shug serves as both an affectionate mentor and a sexual guide for Celie, encouraging her rebellious spirit and helping her envision a new, liberated self.

In this context, Nettie, who has pursued formal education, is profoundly influenced by her teacher, Miss Beasley. Her independent thinking and rebellious spirit are instrumental in her development. Nettie acts as a teacher to her sister Celie, helping her with reading, spelling, and understanding the world beyond their immediate surroundings. Despite their difficult circumstances, Nettie seizes every opportunity to keep Celie informed and engaged with the broader world. During her brief stay in Albert's household with Celie, Nettie's influence and the extraordinary ideas she has absorbed from her education become evident. Celie, buoyed by the hope that Nettie is still alive and that they might reunite, cherishes these memories. In return, Celie provides immense support to Nettie. In the absence of parental care, Celie takes on both the role of sister and surrogate mother, even offering herself to her stepfather to protect Nettie from abuse. Although separated, their deep bond of sisterhood remains a source of strength and hope for both during their most challenging times. Shug Avery initially enters Celie's life as a friend and later becomes her lover, but her influence extends beyond mere companionship. Shug embodies a nurturing, maternal role, guiding Celie with wisdom and care reminiscent of a mother. Through Shug's support, Celie begins her transformation into an independent, self-fulfilled woman, no longer bound by the oppressive conditions that once enslaved her. Celie's first encounter with Shug, brought home by Albert while Shug is gravely ill, marks a pivotal moment. Deprived of maternal affection throughout her life, Celie finds in Shug a protective figure who shields her from Albert's abuse. Shug remains at Albert's house, ensuring that he will no longer harm Celie. In doing so, Shug becomes a guardian angel, helping Celie take her first steps toward independence. This transformative influence is captured in the following lines: "I won't leave, she says, until I know Albert won't even think about beating you." (TCP. 79). Celie first learns about Shug, the woman her husband deeply loves, through a photograph. To Celie, Shug appears as the most beautiful woman she has ever seen, even surpassing her mother in beauty. Celie dedicates herself to caring for Shug during her illness, and Shug is moved by Celie's compassion. In gratitude, Shug composes "Miss Celie's Blues" as a tribute, marking the first time Celie feels respected and acknowledged: "first time somebody made something and named it after me" (TCP 65). This song becomes a significant turning point, sparking the development of their intimate relationship. Their long embrace and kiss signify the deepening of their bond and mark the beginning of their romantic connection. At the start of the novel, Celie lacks a strong female role model to help her assert herself. However, through her interactions with Shug, Celie begins to find the strength she needs to reshape her identity. Celie's experiences of repeated abuse have led her to dissociate from her body, viewing it as something to be rejected to protect herself. To achieve true emancipation, however, a woman must come to understand and accept both her emotional and physical self. As Daniel Ross emphasizes, the journey to reclaim control over one's own body is crucial for personal empowerment and self-assertion:

> One of the primary projects of modern feminism has to restore women's bodies. Because the female body is the most exploited target of male aggression, women have learned to fear or even hate their bodies. Consequently, women often think of their bodies as torn or fragmented, a pattern evident Walker's Celie. To confront the body is to confront not only an individual's abuse but also the abuse of women's bodies through history, as the external symbol of women's enslavement, this abuse represents for women a reminder of her degradation and her consignment to an inferior status."(Ross Pp. 69-83)

With Shug's encouragement, Celie first examines her own body in the mirror and confidently claims it as her own. This moment signifies her initial interest in and appreciation for her body's beauty. Jacques Lacan's theory of the self suggests that self-awareness develops through identification with a significant figure, often the mother, though it can be any consistent nurturer (Ross 77). Celie's growing awareness and admiration of her body through Shug reflect this process of identification. According to Lacan, early in a girl's development, identifying with the mother's body is crucial for accepting one's sexual organs (Ross 77). For Celie, observing Shug's body marks the beginning of this important self-recognition. Although Celie has given birth to two children, she has never experienced sexual pleasure or orgasm. In contrast, Shug leads a liberated and unapologetic sexual life. Shug introduces Celie to the pleasures of sex, and through their intimate encounters, Celie experiences true love for the first time. As Ross notes: Celie's orgasm suggests a rebirth or perhaps an initial birth into a world of love, a re-enactment of the primal pleasure of the child at the mother's breast." (Ross 69)

In her relationship with Shug, Celie discovers a newfound awareness of her sexuality and her body. This relationship is portrayed not as something indecent but as a natural and affectionate connection. Given Celie's history—having only experienced torment and abuse from men—it makes sense that she would not seek out a sexual relationship with a man. In this context, her lesbian relationship with Shug is seen as a preference rather than a matter of biological or genetic orientation. For both women, their union is a first, but it represents a natural progression of their love for one another. At one point, Celie even expresses the sentiment, "We are all lesbians" (Walker 289), which underscores the importance of female friendship and sisterhood within the Black community. The compulsory nature of heterosexuality had previously reinforced Celie's subjugation and erased her sense of self. From the beginning, Celie's life was marked by the shameful secret of incest, leaving her pleading to God for understanding: "Maybe you can give me a sign letting me know what is happening to me" (TCP, 1). For Shug, who recognizes that Celie has never experienced the true pleasures of sex, their relationship is a profound gift of love. For Celie, being loved and engaging in lovemaking completes her spiritual journey toward self-discovery. Upon waking the next morning, Celie feels transformed, recognizing for the first time what it means to be truly loved: "It feels like heaven is what it feels like, not like sleeping with Mr. ___ at all" (TCP, 98). This marks the first time Celie awakens feeling secure and cherished. Shug's initiation of Celie into an awareness of her own body is a crucial step toward her emancipation. By discovering and accepting her body, Celie begins to desire selfhood.

Moreover, when Celie sees her reflection in the mirror, she starts to embrace her new identity. This acceptance empowers her to break free from male domination and to find solace in a community of women. Shug, by listening to Celie's troubles and past traumas, helps her open up emotionally and release the pain and pressure that had silenced her for so long. Celie reflects on this in one of her letters: "My life stop when I left home, I think. But then I think again. It stop with Mr. ___ may be, but start up again with Shug" (TCP, 85). Shug's friendship becomes a lifelong bond that supports Celie through her struggles with Mr. ___ and her painful childhood memories.

When Shug returns to Mr. ___'s house with her new husband Grady, her bond with Celie has grown even stronger. Feeling cold sleeping alone in Grady's absence, Shug joins Celie in bed, and like two schoolgirls, they discuss their sexual experiences. Shug is horrified by Celie's history of sexual abuse and, like a mother, comforts her by wrapping her arms around her, trying to heal her past wounds. For the first time, Celie can respond naturally, shedding tears as she shares her painful story. She reveals that she has never been loved, but Shug reassures her: "I [Shug] love you, Miss Celie." Then, Shug kisses her on the mouth (TCP, 97), solidifying their deep emotional connection.

Sofia's resistance against her father and brother during her youth and unmarried years reveals her strong spirit. Even after marrying, she refuses to accept subjugation or humiliation from her husband, despite her deep love for him. With Shug's support, Sofia begins a successful business stitching trousers, which allows her to achieve financial, physical, and mental independence. Walker crafts Sofia as a resilient character who challenges the oppressive cultural norms for women. She embodies independence and defies patriarchal expectations, striving for gender equality. Celie's journey begins with her enduring the role of a virtual slave, subject to the control of men, traditional sexual roles, racism, and numerous social injustices. Ultimately, she breaks free from these constraints and emerges as a powerful, self-assured woman, transforming into the heroine of her story.

The epistolary novel, which uses letters as its primary narrative method, was a popular form in 18th-century British and European American literature. This form has been particularly appealing to women writers, offering a feminized genre that allows for the expression of their inner selves and the exploration of female identity. Alice Moore Dunbar-Nelson utilized a variation of this form in her unpublished novel, The Confessions of a Lazy Woman (1899), where the female narrator details her neighbors' peculiarities in a diary-like format. A renewed interest in the epistolary form emerged with African American female authors in the late 20th century, highlighting its continued relevance and adaptability. Writers like Alice Walker and Sherley Anne Williams have harnessed the epistolary form or its variations as a foundational element in their novels. *The Color Purple* challenges the traditional Eurocentric male-dominated conventions of the epistolary genre, which has historically been shaped by men to control literary representations of women. By adopting a form historically dominated by men and focusing on women's experiences, Walker asserts her authority and redefines literary images of women, particularly Black women. Her goal is not only to create and control these images but also to give voice to women who have been historically marginalized and silenced.

The epistolary form proves especially effective for exploring the transformative experiences of women, as it allows readers to witness changes in a character's life and mindset through shifts in writing style. Unlike the omniscient narrator of third-person narratives, which provides a comprehensive view of events and characters' inner thoughts, the epistolary form offers a more intimate perspective. Through letters, readers can engage with the character's evolving viewpoints directly. This form also enables the exploration of multiple perspectives, as seen in adaptations like film versions that expand on the experiences of characters beyond Celie and Nettie, such as Sofia, Albert, and Shug.

Slave narratives, which are first-hand accounts of escaped or freed slaves, offer valuable insights into the realities of slavery from the perspective of those who lived through it. These narratives go beyond mere factual recounting to evoke the emotional truths of slavery. Prominent examples, such as Frederick Douglass's Narrative of the Life of Frederick Douglass (1845), played a crucial role in abolitionist literature and influenced the African American literary tradition. Walker's use of the epistolary form in *The Color Purple* aligns with this tradition by allowing Celie to communicate directly with the reader, thus enhancing the authenticity and depth of her story. This approach enables Walker to present multiple perspectives and nuances within the narrative, adding complexity and dimension to the characters and their experiences. Walker's use of anonymity and the epistolary format reflects her literary background and educational influences, showcasing a sophisticated and multifaceted approach to storytelling.

Walker introduces her voice as a poor African American writer using the epistolary form, creating a unique literary space that empowers an uneducated Black Southern woman to express herself. This method allows Celie to write her way into self-awareness and existence. Through the intimate letters of Celie and her sister Nettie, they emerge as real individuals rather than mere fictional characters. The letters, written in idiomatic and colloquial language with direct speech, offer an unfiltered view of their thoughts and emotions, enhancing the sense of immediacy and intimacy. From the start, Celie's writing process reveals the profound impact of her imposed silence and enforced passivity by her husband. Stripped of an emotional and intellectual outlet, she finds solace in writing, which serves as both a therapeutic and liberating practice. The act of journaling provides a genuine escape from her anxieties and a means of self-reflection. Writing becomes a private dialogue between Celie and herself, offering a space for honesty and self-exploration. Through this process, Celie confronts and manages her inner struggles, finding comfort and empowerment in her own words, "When I don't write to you [Nettie] I feel as bad as do when I don't pray." (TCP.110)

Although writing may not erase all of Celie's painful memories, it provides her with a means to manage and gain control over her traumatic experiences, allowing her to distance herself from them. As Wall observes, letter writing offers Celie a powerful tool for processing and overcoming her struggles, "act as a second memory, a projected body that precarious holds[a]hidden self."(Wall 83). Meanwhile, Celie, through her writings understands what is happening to her. For Valerie Babb, writing enables Celie to "fix the events of her life, thereby lending them coherence. Through writing, the protagonist can "review", think and reflect on those events". (Babb 111). In this context, Wendy Wall suggests that "writing serves multiple functions for Celie—it acts as both a symbolic and literal act of rewriting. Through her letters, Celie can define herself in opposition to the patriarchy, and thus...

'reinscribe' those traces and wounds upon her body inflicted and imprinted by others". (Wall 86). In her essay on memory, creation, and writing, Morrison asserts that writing allows individuals to revisit and reconstruct their memories and experiences. She emphasizes the importance for writers to explore the specific context in which events occur and the emotions and impressions they evoke. Morrison defines memory as "the deliberate act of remembering [which] is a form of willed creation" (McConkey 212). This perspective on creative writing encourages writers to examine how and why events are perceived in particular ways.

Literature holds significant power to challenge and transform entrenched ideas. Feminist writers and activists, who recognized this potential, sought to change negative perceptions about women, advocate for gender equality, and highlight injustices faced by women. Their goal was to create a literary world where women could exist as individuals, independent of male perspectives. Throughout history, women have been a central focus in literature, inspiring countless dramatists, novelists, poets, and essayists. However, they have often been portrayed as inferior and passive, existing only through the perspectives of men rather than as individuals in their own right. In recent decades, therapeutic writing has gained prominence not only among healthcare professionals but also in self-improvement circles. Studies in the United States have shown that writing about stressful experiences can lead to significant improvements in mental health, with depressed patients reporting notable benefits after a few months of writing therapy. Alice Walker's writing functions as a form of therapy, particularly in Celie's journey toward emancipation. Walker's commitment to addressing women's struggles is evident in the novel. It portrays a woman who achieves radical change and freedom, offering a message of hope and optimism. The novel serves as an inspiring model for women's liberation.

Celie's letters are a crucial aspect of her therapeutic process. Through her correspondence, she gains insight into her circumstances, questions her situation, and begins to understand herself better. The support from Shug, Nettie, and Sofia is essential to her journey, but writing is equally significant. By expressing herself through letters, Celie gains control over her painful experiences, structures her identity, and finds meaning in her suffering, enabling her to distance herself from trauma. Historically, the feminist contribution in American literature has often been associated with white, middle-class, educated, and heterosexual women. However, African American women writers played a pivotal role in the fight for gender equality long before the 1960s and 1970s. They were influential in both the early feminist movements and the abolitionist movement, demonstrating a strong resistance against patriarchy and advocating for racial and class equality. Their activism and writing have been fundamental in the broader struggle for women's rights.

In the context of feminist theory, Walker's portrayal of Celie celebrates the concept of womanism. The term "womanism," which Alice Walker introduced in her collection In Search of Our Mothers' Gardens: Womanist Prose, is derived from a Black folk expression used by mothers when speaking to their daughters. This concept is encapsulated in the following lines:

> You acting womanish,' i.e. like a woman … usually referring to outrageous, audacious, courageous, or willful behavior. Wanting to know more and in greater depth than is considered 'good' for one … [A womanist is also] a woman who loves other women sexually and/or non-sexually. Appreciates and prefers women's culture … and women's strength … committed to survival and wholeness of entire people, male and female. Not a separatist … Womanist is to feminist as purple is to lavender. (Walker Pp. xi-xii)

The novel charts the evolution of its female protagonist, illustrating the processes of internal organization, disorganization, and reorganization at various levels of human consciousness. It tells the story of a woman whose social constraints shape her behavior and thoughts. As she undergoes emotional and intellectual growth, her psychological transformation leads her to spiritual liberation. *The Color Purple* features a diverse array of female characters, with Celie being distinctly portrayed concerning them. Characters like Nettie, Sophia, Shug Avery, and Harpo's new girlfriend are all Black women, each with unique traits. Celie's specific attitudes and behaviors set her apart, yet they share a common consciousness of their Black womanhood, which influences their sensibilities and binds them together in their struggle against injustice. They all evolve through self-assessment, constantly challenging and revising the roles imposed on them by society. This shared sense of identity fosters solidarity among them, allowing them to confront their collective challenges.

Given the novel's focus on a woman's quest for independence, feminist theories such as radical and socialist feminism offer valuable insights into Celie's behavior and development. Celie's internal journey is depicted through her letters, allowing readers to closely observe her mental growth. It is striking that while Indian society may revere women as embodiments of Goddess Shakti, it simultaneously restricts their roles to narrow confines, limiting their independence. This reflects a broader patriarchal attitude that confines women to rigid roles. Celie's experiences of sexual violence and her resulting low self-esteem, including her inability to share her trauma with her mother and the loss of her children, highlight this societal oppression.

Alice Walker emphasizes the strength women can derive from each other through the relationships depicted in the novel. Celie's empowerment is notably influenced by her interactions with Shug and Sofia, two strong women who assert their rights and fight for justice. Walker demonstrates how collective female solidarity can be a powerful force for empowerment, with Celie drawing strength from it and later helping other women. Celie's development exemplifies womanist growth. She transitions from a young girl constrained by her circumstances into a woman who manages her own business and home, embodying independence and maturity. Her journey reflects a universal perspective and a profound personal transformation. Throughout the novel, themes of hope and despair are prominent. Despite enduring severe sexism and racism, Celie remains resilient and ultimately triumphs. As a Black, poor, and uneducated woman, she manages to liberate herself from patriarchal oppression. By forming supportive relationships with other women, Celie develops a sense of sisterhood and achieves complete independence—spiritually, physically, and economically—by the end of the story. Although *The Color Purple* is a work of fiction, it offers a compelling exploration of moral development, particularly through the character of Celie. Larson observes that by the end of the novel, many of Walker's male characters undergo significant reform. The novel highlights the critical role of female bonding and sisterhood in Celie's journey toward emancipation.

With the support of key female figures—her sister Nettie, her daughter-in-law Sofia, and her husband's mistress Shug—Celie can transform her life and achieve both physical and spiritual liberation. Female relationships in the novel take various forms: some are motherly or sisterly, others mentor-pupil, some are sexual, and others are simply friendships. Sofia attributes her strength to the strong bonds she has with her sisters. Nettie's relationship with Celie provides vital support during her years in Africa. The solidarity among Olinka women helps them endure the challenges of polygamy. Most importantly, Celie's connection with Shug plays a pivotal role in her gradual redemption and self-realization. Walker consistently emphasizes the significance of sisterhood in the empowerment of Black women. She envisions a community of women united as sisters, which can challenge and redefine traditional gender roles. Smith, analyzes the novel by noting that "the unifying bond between Black women is forged through their friendships, love, and shared oppression. This collective strength allows them to break free from their past constraints and build a liberated and equal existence for themselves and their loved ones" (Smith, pp. 181-183). Contrary to the view that sisterhood is merely a rejection of men, it is fundamentally about the spiritual, physical, and material support that women provide each other. This solidarity helps overcome the barriers to women's emancipation and empowerment. A psychological perspective is essential to understanding Celie's mental development, which is central to her journey toward freedom. By examining these aspects, we can address key questions about her growth. The evolution in Celie's writing reflects her psychological state; her letters initially reveal simple thoughts and grammatical errors, indicating her limited understanding of her circumstances. As she grows, her writing style becomes more sophisticated, particularly when she writes to her sister Nettie rather than to God. This shift allows readers to see Celie's transformation as she begins to analyze her feelings and observe those around her. The novel beautifully depicts Celie's evolution from a state of patriarchal oppression to one of awakening and independence.

> Philip Royster censures Walker for "[the] depiction of violent black men who physically and psychologically abuse their wives and children…[and for the] depiction of lesbianism." (Royster 374)

In *The Color Purple*, Alice Walker explores spiritual freedom as a crucial aspect of self-definition. Throughout the novel, Celie's faith undergoes significant transformations. Initially, Celie's understanding of God is shaped by the white, patriarchal interpretations of the Bible. To her, God is depicted as an old, white man with a gray beard, who wears robes and is barefoot—a representation that aligns with her oppressive environment (TCP, p. 165). Celie's obedience to this conception of God leads her to follow directives she believes are divine commands, even at the expense of her desires. For example, when Celie endures sexual abuse and physical violence from her stepfather, she remains silent due to the belief that she must "honor father and mother no matter what" (TCP, p. 39). Her faith in this God, who seems to embody the patriarchal oppression she suffers, leads her to a life of silent submission and resignation.

The turning point in Celie's spiritual journey begins with Nettie's letters, which challenge her previous notions of God. Nettie presents a vision of Jesus as resembling her people, with "hair like lamb's wool," contradicting the white, male image Celie has known. This shift is further reinforced by Shug Avery, who introduces Celie to a more liberating interpretation of spirituality. Shug rejects the traditional church's restrictive views, advocating instead for a personal, less defined concept of God—one that is an impersonal "it" rather than a specific gendered being. She encourages Celie to embrace a spirituality that focuses on personal happiness and appreciation of life's beauty. Shug's perspective helps Celie understand that the essence of life lies in love, admiration, and the enjoyment of beauty and joy. Through these evolving views on God, Celie begins to reject the patriarchal figure she once worshipped, thus achieving a form of spiritual independence and self-empowerment. Celie reflects on her newfound awareness with the realization: "Now that my eyes are opening, I feel like a fool... But as Shug said, you have to get the man off your eyeball before you can see anything clearly" (TCP, p. 168). This insight leads Celie to reject the patriarchal image of God, turning instead towards a love for nature and life itself. In her final letter, she writes: "Dear stars, dear trees, dear sky, dear people, and dear everything. Dear God" (TCP, p. 242).

Celie's progression in understanding God is reflected in her addresses: "Dear stars, dear trees, dear sky, dear people, and dear everything. Dear God" (TCP, p. 242). This shift reveals a profound change in her perception of divinity. She now sees God as an integral part of everything, which transforms her outlook on life and revives her sense of self. Recognizing that she is part of the natural world and that the divine resides within her, Celie experiences genuine redemption and self-realization. This newfound self-love enables her to extend love to others, reflecting Virginia Woolf's notion from *A Room of One's Own* that financial independence and personal space are crucial for a woman's self-expression and autonomy (Woolf, p. 52).

Celie's journey is marked by economic struggle. In her youth, she labors tirelessly in the household and fields, yet owns nothing of her own. Her marriage compounds this, as she and her stepson Harpo work the land, but the harvest benefits only her husband, Albert. Her decision to leave results in her being stripped of everything, reinforcing her subordinate position. Despite her poverty and her husband's refusal to allow her to wear colors she loves, Celie discovers her talent for making pants. With Shug's encouragement, she moves to Memphis, learns the trade, and starts her own business, Folks Pant Unlimited. Sofia also supports her new venture. Economic independence is pivotal for Celie's liberation. It allows her to think freely, unbound by male control. Her manual labor evolves into an artistic pursuit, through which she uncovers her creativity and self-worth. A notable moment occurs when she envisions herself making pants on Shug's dining room floor, affirming her confidence and value as a member of society. Celie's economic autonomy marks a turning point in her life, providing her with a renewed sense of purpose and societal position. Her business empowers her to explore the world on her own terms, without relying on others for interpretation or validation. Thus, sisterhood plays a crucial role in Celie's emancipation. Supported by Nettie, Sofia, and Shug, Celie achieves spiritual and financial freedom, embracing her independence. Throughout this process, her letters serve as a vital tool for her self-discovery and liberation.

On one hand, Celie faces severe abuse, brutality, and dehumanization at the hands of her male oppressors, leaving her with little choice but to remain silent in a harsh, patriarchal world. Despite this, what stands out is Celie's refusal to completely surrender; instead, she chooses to channel her inner turmoil into writing. This act of writing becomes a form of resistance and self-expression in her otherwise oppressive environment. Critics often question the feasibility of Celie's decision.

The skepticism arises from the improbability of an uneducated young Black woman being able to write. This doubt is evident in the following lines: "I can imagine a black woman of Celie's background and education talking with God….but writing letters to God is altogether another matter." (Harris 156)

Although it might seem unlikely for an uneducated Black woman like Celie to write, it is not entirely implausible. Despite being forced to leave school, Celie gains basic literacy skills with the help of her sister, which later supports her writing endeavors. Celie's letters are written in a straightforward style, filled with errors and reflecting her vernacular speech. This demonstrates that for Celie, the act of writing itself is more significant than its form. She embraces her style and words, prioritizing expression over precision. This act of writing empowers Celie with a sense of creativity that extends beyond her letters into new pursuits, such as designing and sewing pants. Alice Walker's dedication to the novel "To the Spirit: Without whose assistance neither this book nor I would have been written" underscores the theme of rebirth through writing. For Celie, writing becomes a means of renewal, enabling her to emerge into a new life. Through her letters, Celie constructs a vibrant, symbolic world that contrasts sharply with the oppressive reality she faces. In her written world, she exercises freedom and explores her desires. This newfound freedom inspires her to challenge and eventually reject the Christian God, whom she views as indifferent to her suffering. By replacing God with her sister Nettie as her confidant, Celie redefines her identity through her writing.

Celie's transformation is evident as her letters evolve from simple notes into more sophisticated reflections. This development mirrors her personal growth and increasing happiness. Her style of writing becomes more formal and expressive, marking a significant shift in her self-awareness and empowerment. Alice Walker acknowledges the influence of Zora Neale Hurston's Their Eyes Were Watching God, noting its importance in her work. Both Walker and Hurston address similar themes and methods in their exploration of Black women's experiences. Hurston's work focuses on the protagonist Janie's journey toward self-discovery and identity, emphasizing the importance of inner voice and personal truth. Both authors highlight the struggle Black women face in finding value and authority within societal and religious structures, advocating for a self-defined sense of self grounded in creative consciousness. In *The Color Purple*, Walker's characters find their strength and wisdom through the support and solidarity of their female community. This contrasts with Hurston's Janie, who, after enduring immense personal hardship, ultimately learns to assert her own identity. Celie's journey culminates in a powerful declaration: "I'm pore, I'm black, I may be ugly and can't cook, ... But I'm here" (TCP 214). This statement signifies her reclamation of self-worth despite the adversities she has faced. Celie's transformation follows a path of physical and emotional suffering, leading her to leave her oppressive husband, Mr. Albert, and finally assert her independence. In this context, Wendy Wall observes: "Throughout The Color Purple, inherent biological gender characteristics are questioned; gender becomes a socially-imposed categorization."(Wall Pp 83-97)

Walker also introduces the art of quilt-making, which she herself works on while she writes the novel: "I bought some beautiful blue-and-red-and purple fabric ... My quilt began to grow. And, of course, everything was happening. Celie and Shug and Albert were getting to know each other." (Walker 358). Quilting in *The Color Purples* serves as a powerful symbol of female bonding, sisterhood, and unity. Walker's depiction of quilting reflects her deep respect and affection for Black cultural traditions. She highlights a quilt displayed at the Smithsonian, created by "an anonymous Black woman from Alabama," noting that this unnamed artist was "one of our grandmothers—an artist who left her mark with the only materials she could afford and in the only medium permitted by her social position" (Walker 239). For Alice Walker, quilting represents the creative legacy passed down from African American foremothers. It embodies the artistry and spiritual depth of those who transformed humble scraps into meaningful works. Through quilting, Walker underscores the profound imagination and resilience of these women, who used their limited resources to create enduring art that reflects their heritage and creative spirit.

> "Weaving, shaping, sculpting or quilting in order to create a kaleidoscopic and momentary array is tantamount to providing an improvisational response to chaos. It constitutes survival strategy and motion in the face of dispersal. A patchwork quilt, laboriously and affectionately crafted from bits of worn overalls, shredded uniforms, tattered petticoats, and outgrown dresses stands as a signal instance of a patterned wholeness in the African Diaspora." (Walker 239)

Celie's passivity in *The Color Purple* is often met with skepticism, as Trudier Harris finds it difficult to accept that a young Black woman could be so submissive. Harris challenges the plausibility of Celie's inaction, pointing out that even enslaved women historically found ways to resist, such as running away, sabotaging their masters' food, or otherwise fighting back (Harris Pp. 155-161). However, Harris's perspective may overlook the broader context of slavery's impact on resistance. Historical accounts show that the brutality and dehumanization experienced by African slaves often led to profound psychological and physical trauma. Enslaved individuals, subjected to severe punishment and systematic oppression from the moment they were captured and transported to

America, were frequently stripped of their autonomy and spirit. The relentless abuse and indoctrination transformed many from free individuals into docile and subdued beings, compelled to adopt a 'slave identity' characterized by fearfulness and passivity. Celie's passivity, therefore, can be seen as a reflection of the deep psychological scars inflicted by such an oppressive system, rather than an anomaly. Her journey towards self-assertion is a testament to the resilience required to overcome such profound conditioning. In her book, *Ain't I A Woman black women and feminism*, Bell Hooks explains

> "a slavery in order to make his product (a slave) saleable, he has to ensure that this male or female slave would react. The prideful, arrogant and independent spirit of the African people had to be 157 broken so that they would conform to the white colonizer's notion of proper slave demeanor" (Hooks Pp. 450-470)

Similarly, Celie, a poor and uneducated African American girl, exemplifies hope through her resilience, faith, and courage. Her journey illustrates how crucial female bonding is for achieving liberation. For example, her sister Nettie, who serves as a teacher and a beacon of hope, helps Celie channel her suffering into writing. Sofia, acting as a mentor, profoundly influences Celie's awakening of her rebellious spirit. Sofia's bravery and independence inspire Celie to envision a life beyond her oppressive circumstances and catalyze her transformation. Shug's role in helping Celie recognize and embrace her own body is pivotal to her journey toward self-discovery and independence. By seeing herself clearly and accepting her body, Celie starts to desire a new sense of self, which allows her to break free from male dominance and build her identity through female relationships. Sisterhood proves essential to Celie's emancipation, enabling her to liberate herself spiritually, physically, and economically. Her connections with Nettie, Sofia, and Shug become lifelong bonds that support her emotional healing and personal growth. Shug's redefinition of 'God' as a source of love, beauty, and joy helps Celie gain confidence and recognize her power.

Celie's path to freedom intertwines with her writing. While Shug and Nettie assist in her spiritual and emotional liberation, Celie's writing serves as a critical tool for self-assertion. Through her letters, she begins to confront her abuser and reclaim her identity, which is instrumental in her journey toward economic independence and self-empowerment. Writing fosters a sense of creativity and self-worth, complementing the support she receives from the women around her. Alice Walker's novel also envisions a model for ideal relationships between men and women. It advocates for women to stand up against injustice and to support one another. Despite competing interests, the women in the novel unite to sustain each other. Their struggles ultimately lead to their happiness and empowerment.

The novel's message extends beyond black women, encouraging all oppressed women to fight for their independence and challenge patriarchal dominance. As Walker suggests, true change begins in the mind, and like Celie, women must fight for their transformation to achieve freedom and establish equitable relationships with men. Indeed, the history of patriarchy is marked by widespread injustices, with women enduring systemic oppression under male dominance. This system, driven by male self-interest, has stifled women's full development as human beings. Under patriarchy, sexism is the prevailing norm, with men maintaining control over all aspects of life, thereby perpetuating women's subjugation and denying them equal power. As a result, women are often deprived of their fundamental rights and are excluded from social, political, and economic spheres. Simone de Beauvoir, in *The Second Sex,* argues that women are defined in relation to men, with men positioned as the primary subjects and women as the secondary, suffering "Other." This perspective reinforces the notion that women are inherently less capable, reinforcing their subservience and marginalization. Such biased and inaccurate portrayals undermine women's dignity and identity, relegating them to a subordinate role based on imposed cultural and social constraints rather than their actual capacities.

Alice Walker, a prominent Black American writer, vividly portrays the impact of patriarchy through her own experiences and uses writing as a means of confronting and overcoming her traumatic past. Her novel reflects her struggles and growth, highlighting her journey toward emancipation and success as an influential author. The dedication of her work to her life, career, and education underscores her commitment to addressing and overcoming the injustices she faced. Charles Larson, in his Detroit News Review of *The Color Purple*, emphasizes... "I wouldn't go as far as to say that all the male characters [in the novel] are villains, but the truth is fairly close to that". (Larson 35). Subsequently Peter S.Prescott joins Ford's opinion declaring in a Newsweek review

"I want to say, that The Color Purple is an American novel of permanent importance, that rare sort of book which diversion in the fields of dread". (Prescott 1982: 676)

Prescott highlights that *The Color Purple* establishes Alice Walker among the great American writers, such as William Faulkner. Walker is noted for her commitment to literature that serves a purpose beyond mere artistic expression, which is evident in *The Color Purple*. The novel not only portrays the harsh realities of racism and sexism faced by African American women but also offers potential solutions and pathways to overcome these adversities and achieve a better life. Despite its acclaim, the novel has been met with both praise and criticism from a diverse array of reviewers, including black and white, male and female critics.

Andrea Ford, writing for the Detroit Free Press, praises Walker's work, calling it "a jewel of a novel" (35-38). Similarly, David Guy's review in the Washington Post Book World commends the novel's portrayal of women who, by accepting themselves, manage to escape oppression and build independent lives (Guy 7). However, some critics argue against the novel's prominence, suggesting that it presents an overly idealized and unrealistic narrative. There are concerns that Walker's depiction of black males is unfairly negative and misleading. Robert Towers, for instance, critiques the novel for its portrayal of black men and its utopian elements, "Walker for the creation of an unrealistic plot". (Towers Pp. 35-36). The novel vividly recounts the extensive abuse—sexual, emotional, and physical—that Celie endures from her stepfather throughout her life. This grim portrayal of Celie's suffering highlights the oppressive, patriarchal culture that relegates women to a subservient role. In her community, women are expected to remain invisible, never making eye contact with men, and are valued only through their usefulness to their husbands. Celie, isolated and vulnerable, cannot confide in her family about her trauma. Her stepfather denies her education, repeatedly assaults her, and systematically destroys her self-esteem. Despite being the victim, Celie internalizes a sense of defilement and corruption. Walker uses Celie's experience to reflect on the broader plight of defenseless black women.

This situation parallels the experiences of many Indian women, as depicted in the works of Girish Karnad. His plays reveal how male protagonists attempt to control and condition women's minds within a society that maintains that women must remain subordinate—from childhood under their fathers' authority, to their husbands during their youth, and eventually to their sons in old age. However, *The Color Purple* resonates with a diverse readership beyond its specific historical context. Its exploration of family dynamics, emotional experiences, sexual relationships, and fantasy appeals to women across various backgrounds. Walker has observed how entrenched divisions in psychic and social life perpetuate gender and racial inequalities. In contrast to Celie's early victimization, her evolution into a fully realized, modern woman represents a significant shift. Alice Walker's novel is a landmark in black fiction for its comprehensive critique of patriarchal domination within the black community. Walker's work represents a unique decolonization of traditional notions of love. As traditional forms of love—within family, community, or nation—fail to provide safety and fulfillment, Walker advocates for a redefined understanding of love. Her narrative illustrates that both religion and marriage have fallen short in fostering genuine love, particularly impacting women most profoundly.

Walker suggests that the solution to this crisis lies in transforming traditional concepts of love. She demonstrates that, despite the failures of conventional institutions, love remains a crucial redeeming force. Through Celie's journey from childhood trauma to self-realization, the novel explores the impact of familial violence on identity and highlights her path to self-awareness and independence.

Works Cited

Babb, Valerie. "Writing Selves in The Color Purple." *Studies in American Fiction*, vol. 18, no. 1, 1990, pp. 111-118.

Ford, Andrea. "A Jewel of a Novel." *Detroit Free Press*, 1982, pp. 35-38.

Guy, David. "Escaping Oppression: A Review of The Color Purple." *Washington Post Book World*, 1982, p. 7.

Harris, Trudier. *From Mammies to Militants: Domestics in Black American Literature*. Temple UP, 1982.

Hooks, Bell. *Ain't I a Woman: Black Women and Feminism*. South End Press, 1981.

Larson, Charles. "A Review of The Color Purple." *Detroit News Review*, 1982, p. 35.

McConkey, James. "Memory and Creation in Writing." *New York Review of Books*, vol. 34, no. 4, 1987, pp. 210-212.

McDowell, Deborah. "The Epistolary Character of The Color Purple." *Signs: Journal of Women in Culture and Society*, vol. 12, no. 2, 1987, pp. 281-302.

Morrison, Toni. "Memory, Creation, and Writing." *Literary Studies Journal*, vol. 21, 1987, pp. 212-218.

Prescott, Peter S. "The Color Purple: An American Novel of Permanent Importance." *Newsweek*, 1982, p. 676.

Ross, Daniel W. "The Body as a Site of Resistance in The Color Purple." *Feminist Studies in Literature*, vol. 14, no. 1, 1990, pp. 69-83.

Royster, Philip. "Depiction of Violence in Walker's The Color Purple." *African American Review*, vol. 22, 1988, pp. 374-378.

Smith, Barbara. "Black Women's Friendships in The Color Purple." *Feminist Literary Studies*, vol. 9, no. 2, 1991, pp. 181-183.

Towers, Robert. "Walker's Utopian Vision in The Color Purple." *New York Times Book Review*, 1982, pp. 35-36.

Walker, Alice. *The Color Purple*. Harcourt Brace Jovanovich, 1982.

Wall, Wendy. "Writing as Resistance in The Color Purple." *Journal of Feminist Studies*, vol. 15, 1993, pp. 83-97.

Washington, Mary Helen. "Alice Walker: A Study of Her Works." *Feminist Studies in Literature*, vol. 7, no. 1, 1985, pp. 133-139.

Woolf, Virginia. *A Room of One's Own*. Harcourt Brace, 1929.

Bibliography

Angelou, Maya. *I Know Why the Caged Bird Sings*. Bentham Books, 1971.

Achille, Louis Th, "The Negroes and Art", *La Revuedumondenoir 1*, pp.57.

Alexandra, Lillehei. *"Pigments in Translation"* (Senior Thesis, Wesleyan College, 2011). 78, accessed, 4Dec. 2020, http:// wesscholar. wesleyan. edu/ cgi/ view content. cgi/ article1705 &context.etdhon theses.

Abbott, Porter H. *The Cambridge Introduction to Narrative. Cambridge* University Press, 2002.

Boas, Franz. *Race, Language, Culture*. Houghton Mifflin, 1959.

Boyd, Valerie. *Wrapped in Rainbows: The Life oHurstonNeale Hurtson*. Scribner, 200Hurstonley, Keith and Paul Cartledge. *The Cambridge World History of Slavery; The Ancient Mediterranean World. Vol. I.* Cambridge University Press, 2011.

Collins, Patricia. *Black Feminist Thought: Knowledge Consciousness and the Politics of Empowerment*. Unurin Hayman, 1990.

Campbell, Josie P. *Students Companion to Zora Neale Hurston*. GreenWood Press, 2001.

Equiano, Olaudah. *The Interesting Narrative of the Life of Olaudah Equiano or Gustavus Vassa.* Printed for, and sold by the author, 1974.

Edward, Brent Hayes. *The Practice of Diaspora: Literature, Translation and the Rise of Black Internationalism.* Harvard University Press, 2003.

Foster, Frances & Smith and Larose, Davis. *Early African American Women's Literature* Cambridge University Press, 2009.

Hughes, Carl Milton. *The Negro Novelist: A Discussion of the Writing of American Negro Novelists* 1940-1950, the Citadel Press, 1970.

Jordan, June. "Notes towards a Balancing of Love and Hatred". *Black World* 24:10 Aug1974.

Jones, Gayl. *Liberating Voices: Oral Tradition in African American Literature.* Harvard University Press, 1991.

King, Deborah. "Multiple Jeopardy, Multiple Consciousness: The Context of Lack Feminist Ideology." *Feminist Ideology Anthology of African American Thought.* Ed. Guy Sheftall. New Press, 1985.

Kulkarni, Harihar. *Black Feminist Fiction: A March Towards Liberation.* Creative Books, 1999.

Kahnweiler, Henry Daniel. "L'ArtNegreetleCubime", *Presence Africaine 3.* pp.370,

Kesteloot, Lilyan. *Black Writers in French: A Literary History of Negritude, trans. Ellen Conroy Kennedy.* Temple University Press, 1974.

Kennedy and Convrov, E llen.The Negritude Poets; an anthology of translations from the French. The Viking Pre, 1975.